The
MOST
WONDERFUL
MOVIE
in the
WORLD

The
MOST WONDERFUL MOVIE
in the
WORLD

BARBARA FORD

Dutton Children's Books
New York

CIP Data is available.

Published in the United States 1996 by
Dutton Children's Books,
a division of Penguin Books USA Inc.
375 Hudson Street, New York, New York 10014

Designed by Lilian Rosenstreich

Printed in U.S.A.
First Edition
2 4 6 8 10 9 7 5 3 1
ISBN 0-525-45455-1

The
MOST
WONDERFUL
MOVIE
in the
WORLD

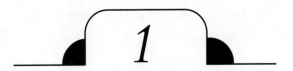

Moira opened the big book on her dressing table. She read it as she dressed.

> *"Mrs. Charles Hamilton—one hundred and fifty dollars —in gold."*

Moira gasped, pulling on her shorts. This was so exciting! Would she do it? Would she dance with him?

"Moira! Are you up?" Her mother's voice came from outside the bedroom door. The voice seemed far away, because Moira was at the ball with Scarlett, waiting to see what Rhett would do next.

"Moira! Are you up?"

"Yes!"

"Well, come down to breakfast. It's after nine."

Sighing, Moira put her pencil back in the book to mark her place. She still had a long way to go, even though she had read almost two hundred pages already. *Gone With the Wind* was so long! But it was so exciting. She stuck a handkerchief in the pocket of her shorts. It was the allergy season, and she had to have a handkerchief ready at all times. Then, carrying the book, she ran down the stairs. Her mother was in the kitchen.

"An egg?" asked Mrs. Flynn.

"Toast and jam. Peach jam." Mrs. Flynn had made peach jam from the peaches on their tree. Moira set the book on the kitchen table and opened it.

"How far are you?"

"I'm at the part where she's a widow and she's all in black and she's at the party, and he says he'll pay a hundred and fifty dollars in gold to dance with her and he won't dance with anybody else!"

"I read that part over and over." Her mother smiled. "Do you like the book?"

Moira looked at her mother. "It's the most wonderful book I've ever read," she breathed.

"Everybody says that. But it's an awfully long book for an eleven-year-old. Over a thousand pages!" Mrs. Flynn put two slices of bread in the toaster. "I heard the movie's finally coming to the Lebanon Theater for a week. They're going to charge extra for it. The center section will be all reserved seats."

4

"Oh, Mom! When?"

"Next month. It took almost two years to get here. You remember they had the world premiere in Atlanta in 1939."

Moira nodded. The pictures of the premiere had been in *Life* magazine. Vivien Leigh, the actress who played Scarlett, was there. She was the most beautiful woman Moira had ever seen. Black hair. Green eyes. White skin. And now the movie with Vivien Leigh in it was coming here to Lebanon!

"Mom—can I see it, *please?*"

"You know what the Legion of Decency says, Moira. *Gone With the Wind* is 'Objectionable in Part for All.' That makes it a B." Mrs. Flynn put the toast and peach jam in front of Moira. "Don't get any jam on the pages."

Every week, the Legion of Decency had a list of movies in church newspapers all across the country. The ones children could see were under the heading A-1, and the ones adults could see were under A-2. Nobody was supposed to see the ones under B or, of course, C. C meant "Condemned." But practically all Condemned movies were made in countries where people didn't even speak English, so nobody here wanted to see them anyway.

B movies were different. Some good movies were under B. And so was the most wonderful movie in the world, *Gone With the Wind.*

5

"Mom, I didn't make the Legion of Decency pledge last year in church! I was sick, remember?"

"It doesn't make any difference. I won't send a child of mine off to see a B movie—a movie I would not even see myself."

"Oh, Mom! I'm already reading the book!"

"There's no Legion of Decency for books," said Mrs. Flynn. "I've got to see about the wash."

Moira heard her mother's quick footsteps running down the basement steps. It wasn't fair! *Gone With the Wind* was *finally* coming to Lebanon, almost two years after it opened, and she couldn't see it because she was a Catholic. Why couldn't she be a Unitarian like her best friend, Jane? Jane could see any movie she wanted to, practically.

She held the handkerchief to her nose just in time. *Achoooo!*

The kitchen door opened. Mr. Flynn came in carrying a basket of tomatoes. "Best year we've had for tomatoes since we moved here. Look at these!"

"Um," said Moira, sniffing. She opened the book again. It had fallen closed when she sneezed. Where was she?

"You have one of these tomatoes for lunch, Moira. Nothing like a bacon, lettuce, and tomato sandwich on toast."

"Okay, Daddy." She hoped he wouldn't be around when she was eating lunch because she didn't want another tomato. She must have eaten a million already this year. Her mother had even put one in her lunch yesterday. She was going to throw it in the trash but then she saw her teacher, Sister Gabriel Mary, looking at her, so she had to eat it. It squirted on her blouse, and Mary Lou Prezwalski laughed.

Mr. Flynn set the basket down and picked up a tomato. He held it up admiringly. "Look at that color!"

"Daddy, the movie *Gone With the Wind,* it's finally coming to the Lebanon Theater. It took almost two years to get here! I want to see that movie so much!"

"That so?" Mr. Flynn began to wash the tomato.

"But Mom says I can't because it's a B."

"It's a sin to see a B," said Mr. Flynn, picking up another tomato.

She might have known her father would agree with her mother about B movies. About the only thing they agreed on was what she couldn't do. "Daddy? I'm already reading the book, see?" Moira held up the book. "So why can't I see the movie?"

"Why do you want to see a movie with a made-up story like that? If you want to see a movie, you come down to the office some day next week, and I'll take you to the newsreel theater again."

"Oh, Daddy! I don't want to see a *newsreel.* I want to see *Gone With the Wind.* It's the greatest movie ever made! It won ten Academy Awards!"

"I saw a newsreel last week on the war in North

7

Africa," said Mr. Flynn. "That General Rommel, he's beating those English there again, just like he did in France. Serves them right."

Moira didn't say anything. If you said anything at all, he just talked more about how awful the English were. A long time ago, her father's family had lived in Ireland. So had her mother's family, but they didn't talk so much about it. Anyway, a long, long time ago, England had conquered Ireland and made it part of England. England had given most of Ireland back by now, but her father was still mad. He liked to see people pushing England around.

She searched for her place in the book. Here it was. Scarlett was going to dance with Rhett to raise money for the Confederate soldiers in the Civil War! The Civil War sounded lots more interesting than the war in Europe. Or North Africa. Those places were so far away.

"Where's your mother?" asked Mr. Flynn, turning off the faucet. The tomatoes now marched across the windowsill in a long red line.

"Basement."

"You tell your mother I have lots more tomatoes and I'll pick some kale for tonight," he said. Picking up the empty basket, he went out the kitchen door.

Last night, Moira had started a drawing of Scarlett in a green dress. She'd finish it today. She headed down the basement steps. Her mother was feeding a sheet though the wringer on the washing machine. The water the wringer squeezed out ran into the wash-tub.

"More tomatoes," groaned Mrs. Flynn when Moira delivered her message.

"And kale," said Moira. "I hate kale, Mom."

"You've got to help eat it! We've got tons of it! I'll put that sauce you like on it," she added in a softer tone.

Moira skipped into the recreation room. Mr. Flynn had walled off half of the basement to make the rec room, and Mrs. Flynn had supplied some old pieces of furniture. Moira's art supplies were in a metal cabinet: paper, pencils, an art-gum eraser, a watercolor paint set, a jar of brushes, another jar for water. She set these items on the table. There was a paper doll on the table already—Vivien Leigh as Scarlett. A long green dress was fixed to her body with little paper tabs.

Moira examined the doll's small, perfect face with its pointed chin and cloud of black hair. The green gown matched the doll's eyes. Vivien Leigh was so beautiful!

In her drawing, Scarlett was standing in front of her big house with the white pillars. It had a name: Tara. She knew just what Tara looked like, because the paper-doll book Scarlett came from had a picture of Tara on the front. Besides, *Life* magazine had printed pictures from the movie when it first came out. She had cut out every single picture and saved them.

She held up the drawing. Last night, she had been pleased with it. But today she saw flaws everywhere. Weren't Scarlett's arms too short? And weren't the pillars of the house crooked? She sat down at the table and picked up the eraser.

By the time she finished, the whole paper was covered with eraser crumbs, but it was worth it. Scarlett's arms ended where arms should end. The pillars were straight enough to hold up the mansion. She was ready to paint.

She filled the jar with water at the washtubs. Back at the table, she dipped the brush in the jar and then rubbed the brush over the green paint.

"That's a good drawing, Moira!" said her mother behind her. "Scarlett O'Hara in front of Tara."

"This is my favorite dress. Mom, when did she wear it?"

"It was after the Civil War was over. Scarlett is very poor, even though they still have Tara. So she takes down the living room drapes and makes them into this beautiful green velvet dress."

Upstairs, there was a faint ringing. "You get it, Moira," said Mrs. Flynn. "You haven't started painting the dress yet."

Moira set the brush full of green paint carefully

against the water jar and flew up the stairs. The phone was in the hall on the first floor. "H'lo?"

"*Gone With the Wind* is coming to the Lebanon Theater!" cried her friend Jane's voice.

"I know." Moira could feel her heart dive like one of those planes that got shot down on the newsreels. *Eeeeeeeeeeeeeeee.* She knew what Jane was going to say next.

"My parents are taking me to see it! On Saturday night! That's the best time!"

Moira held the phone away from her ear so that all she could hear was a tiny little voice saying something she couldn't understand.

Jane wasn't even reading *Gone With the Wind*. Vivien Leigh wasn't even her favorite actress. It wasn't fair that Jane got to see the movie and she didn't!

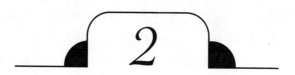

Clutching their tickets, Moira and and Jane made their way through the crowd of children in the lobby of the Lebanon Theater. It was Saturday afternoon, when the Lebanon held its matinee for children. Moira and Jane went almost every week.

"Look!" said Moira, pointing. "Pictures from *Gone With the Wind!*"

They pushed their way to the case. Most movies were in black and white, of course, but the pictures from *Gone With the Wind* were in color. And what color! "That's the green velvet dress," murmured Moira, her nose against the glass. "It's just . . . beautiful."

"Who's that?" asked Jane, pointing to a photograph of a tall, thin blond man in a uniform who was looking down at Scarlett.

"It must be Ashley," said Moira. "He goes in the army."

"He's cute," said Jane. "But not as cute as Clark Gable."

Moira stared at the photograph of the thin blond man playing Ashley. She remembered his name from *Life* magazine—Leslie Howard. But she had never noticed before that he looked like somebody she knew. Who?

By the time they had studied all the photographs, the theater doors were open. "Come on, we've got to get good seats," said Jane.

This time it was Moira's turn to choose the seats, so they sat in the first two on the side aisle, halfway down. These were her favorite seats. In the outside seat, there was never anybody in front of you.

"I'll get the popcorn," said Moira.

By the time she came back, the theater was almost full. As soon as she sat down, Moira began to feel excited. The feature today, she knew, was just a movie with Judy Garland that she'd already seen. But when the thick red drapes in front of the screen moved back and the room went dark except for the screen, everything would change. It would be like you had moved right into that world on the screen.

And it was such an exciting world! People were bigger and more beautiful there and they wore clothes that fit perfectly and never wrinkled. Their hair always looked like they had just fixed it. The way people spoke and did things up there on the screen was so much better than the way real people did them, too. In the screen world, people always knew what to say and how to move around without bumping into things.

Judy Garland could even make hard things like dancing and singing at the same time look easy.

"It's two o'clock," observed Jane. "They're going to be late again."

At 2:05, the red curtains in front of the screen still hadn't moved. Somebody in the back began to stamp. Others joined in. Soon the whole audience was stamping, Moira and Jane along with the rest.

Then, all of a sudden, from the back of the theater came a beam of light, a beam of light with a million little pieces of dust dancing inside it. There was something on the screen now, something you could see through the red drapes. The drapes slowly moved to each side.

"And now, the March of Time!" The familiar music pounded through the theater.

"This is always so *boring*," whispered Jane. "Why don't they just show the movie?"

Moira dug her hand into the popcorn box again. There were pictures on the screen of people walking down a street with lots of tall buildings, then pictures of people sitting in a drugstore. "To the United States in the year 1941, to its villages and its towns and cities, has come a growing realization of how near to the American community is war," droned the March of Time voice.

Then President Roosevelt was on the screen, speaking in that familiar voice. "Let us say to the democracies, 'We are vitally concerned in your defense of freedom. We shall send you, in ever increasing numbers, ships, planes, tanks, guns. That is our purpose and that is our policy!' "

Some people in the audience clapped. Others hissed.

"My father said President Roosevelt never should have got the third term," whispered Jane. "Now he thinks he can do *anything.*"

Moira didn't answer. Jane's parents were Republicans, like most of the people in Lebanon. Republicans didn't like anything President Roosevelt did, because he was a Democrat. The Flynns were Democrats, but her father said they shouldn't talk about it.

A line of big ships had appeared on the screen. "Fifty U.S. destroyers have been turned over to Britain under the Lend-Lease program and have become units of the Royal Navy," said the March of Time voice.

"Against the assaults of tyranny, England still exists—and every day grows stronger and stronger! Time . . . marches on!"

The newsreel was finally over. And now, with a burst of familiar music, something new was on the screen.

PREVIEWS OF COMING ATTRACTIONS
David O. Selznick's Masterpiece

Moira sat up. David O. Selznick! She had seen that name somewhere. And she had heard that music on the radio. It was such beautiful music it made you want to cry.

GONE WITH THE WIND

As the words spilled across the screen, Moira gasped.

"A movie so thrilling, so charged with human emotions, that it will sweep you into the pages of history," throbbed a man's voice. And then Vivien Leigh was there, running right at the screen and wearing a long, full white dress with little green flowers on it. Moira had never seen anyone so beautiful!

"It's *her*," whispered Moira, grabbing Jane's arm. "And that's the dress she wore at the barbecue! That was where she met Rhett!"

Now Vivien Leigh was all in black, dancing with a tall man with a black mustache—the scene at the ball, after Rhett paid the hundred and fifty dollars in gold! And now she was sitting in a wagon with flames behind her. And now she was running down a road, her arms out, toward a man, another man. Ashley? Yes. And now she was kissing him in front of a sunset redder than the flames. Moira put her hand to her lips. Would anyone ever kiss *her* like that? The boys in her class never even looked at her.

Scarlett was in green now—the beautiful long-sleeved green gown she'd made out of the curtains! This time she was kissing Rhett. Rhett was good-looking, all right. But she liked the way Ashley looked better, with his pale face and pale hair and pale eyes that seemed to look right into Scarlett.

Moira sank back as the music crashed and words flashed on the screen.

LIMITED ENGAGEMENT
OCTOBER 15–21
Reserved Seats Available

"Do you think Vivien Leigh's as pretty as Linda Darnell?" asked Jane.

Moira turned to look at Jane with amazement. She couldn't be serious! "*Much* prettier," said Moira.

She didn't pay much attention to the movie that

followed the previews. You could see Judy Garland and the other Hollywood stars anytime. Vivien Leigh was going to be here for only a limited engagement. And I won't be able to see her, thought Moira.

After the movie was over, Moira followed Jane into the lobby, replaying the scenes from the preview in her mind. Scarlett ran and danced and kissed and kissed again.

"Did you like the feature?" asked Jane.

"What?" said Moira, moving through the barbecue with Scarlett. How she'd love to wear a dress like Scarlett's at the barbecue, a long white dress with little flowers on it.

"Wake up, Moira! I asked if you liked the movie we just saw. With Judy Garland, remember? She *used* to be your favorite star."

"Oh, yeah." She couldn't remember anything about the Judy Garland movie. Judy Garland was cute. But Vivien Leigh, who was Scarlett, was beautiful. No wonder everybody kissed Scarlett. No wonder everybody was in love with Scarlett. Moira frowned as she saw herself in a lobby mirror. Would anyone ever be in love with *her?*

One of the boys in the lobby looked familiar. A pale face, light hair, freckles. Ronald Colligan. Ronald Colligan from her class. She dropped her eyes. She never said hello to any of the boys. And they never said hello to her. They saved their hellos for girls like

Mary Lou Prezwalski, the prettiest girl in the seventh grade.

"Hello, Moira."

He had said hello! And he knew her name! Astonished, Moira raised her eyes to Ronald's. He had light-colored eyes. Gray? "Hello," she mumbled. Ronald, she suddenly realized, looked like somebody. Leslie Howard! Ronald looked like the man who played Ashley! Ashley, the man Scarlett *really* loved! Ashley, who was so much cuter than Rhett!

Ronald was going out the door now with an older boy.

"Who's that boy who talked to you? He's kind of cute." Jane stared after the two boys.

"A boy in my class. My new teacher, Sister Gabriel Mary, she says he's the worst boy in both seventh grades."

They were outside the theater, blinking in the bright sunlight.

"What does he *do?*" Jane wanted to know as they walked toward the bus stop.

"One thing he does is imitate Sister." Moira giggled. "It's funny. Sister is mean. She has this tiny little smile you can hardly see."

Jane looked sympathetic. "Nuns are weird," she said. "I'm glad we don't have any at our school. Do you like St. Teresa's any better now you're in seventh grade?"

Moira shook her head. "It's just the same. The girls have all known each other forever. They all live near the school."

"All of them?"

"There are a couple who walk from Dorchester. The others live right around the school. They all do things together. I'm the only one who takes the bus, the only one who lives in Sunrise Hills."

In her mind, she saw herself get off the Sunrise Hills bus and go down the long walk to the school, all alone. She saw herself standing in the school yard, all alone. No one spoke to her. No one even noticed her. When she went to St. Teresa's, she left the familiar world of Jane and the other kids they played games with and her parents and the neighbors and her house. She left all that and went into a whole different world. In that world, she was nobody.

"St. Teresa's is like . . . like another world," she said, struggling to describe it. "And there's no place for me there, like there is at home. Maybe if I was good at jump rope . . ."

Jane grabbed Moira's arm and swung it back and forth. "I wish you could go to my school. It wouldn't matter if you were good at jump rope."

"Yeah," said Moira. It would be so nice to go to the school near her house. It was only six blocks away. And she'd start out with one big advantage: friends. But Catholic kids had to go to Catholic schools. Not sending your kids to Catholic schools was a sin. So when she was ready to go into fifth grade, Daddy had said she was old enough to take the bus to the Catholic school.

They were at the bus stop. Jane continued to swing Moira's arm. "And I wish you could go see *Gone With the Wind,*" said Jane.

"I'm going to see it," said Moira. The words surprised her. She didn't know she was going to say them. But now that they were said, she knew they were the right words. "I'm going," she repeated.

Jane had stopped swinging Moira's arm. "You can't go with *us.* I already told my mother your mother says you can't go, so my mother won't take you."

"I know. I'm going myself."

"When?"

"I don't know."

"It's only here for a week. It starts October fifteenth."

"I know."

The Sunrise Hills bus rolled to a stop in front of them.

"General admission's only a dollar," said Jane as they sat down inside the bus. "But you have to sit in the side seats."

"They're my favorites!"

Jane talked about a lot of things as the bus carried them home. But Moira had trouble listening. Her

21

own thoughts got in the way. She had never seen a movie by herself before. She had never seen a B movie before. She had never seen a movie without her parents knowing she went. But that wasn't all. Seeing it would be a sin. And lying about it to her parents— another sin!

Sometimes there seemed to be sins all around you. But she had to see it. Because it was the most wonderful movie in the world.

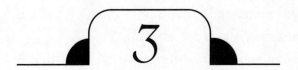

Yawning, Moira padded barefoot into the bathroom. "No water," she reminded herself. Last Sunday morning, she had drunk a glass of water before she remembered that she was going to Communion. The water broke her fast, so she couldn't go. She swallowed. Already, her mouth felt dry.

A half hour later, she was dressed for church. She looked at herself in the big mirror in her mother and father's room. Her mother had bought the dress on sale, and it was a funny color blue. Her blue hat didn't match it, either. Under the hat, her long hair drooped.

She wiggled her nose. It itched. She didn't have a handkerchief with her, so she ran back to her room.

"Remember your gloves!" her mother shouted up the stairs just as Moira sneezed.

"And an extra handkerchief!" added the voice from downstairs.

Where were her white gloves? She pulled open her top drawer with such force that the picture of Vivien Leigh as Scarlett, the picture she'd cut out of *Life* magazine and put in a frame, fell over. She righted the picture, then searched the drawer. No gloves. She put an extra handkerchief in her purse.

"I can't find my gloves," she announced as she ran down the steps.

Mrs. Flynn, who wore a green suit and a green hat that perched on top of her upswept hair, frowned. She held her own white gloves in her hand. "You need gloves for church."

"I can't find them."

"Well, we have to go now. I was so embarrassed when we came in late last week. Father Monahan was ready to give the gospel and he looked right at me. Of course he goes so fast that he gets to the gospel in no time. Dave! Can we leave now?"

Mr. Flynn appeared, jiggling his car keys. He always went to the seven o'clock mass because crowds made him nervous. Then he drove Moira and her mother to the ten o'clock mass.

As the car went down the street, Moira felt another sneeze coming on. She tried to stifle it with the handkerchief, but it was no use. That sneeze was followed by a whole series of sneezes, each one like a little explosion.

"I saw all the goldenrod out in the field behind the house," said Mrs. Flynn, looking back at her daughter. "That's why you're having trouble."

Moira, eyes watering over the handkerchief, nodded. Goldenrod was the one of the things she was most allergic to.

"How was the sermon?" Mrs. Flynn asked her husband.

"That priest from the college gave it again. Can't understand him. But it was short. They had the Legion of Decency pledge today."

Moira leaned forward. "What, Daddy?" she asked through her handkerchief.

"I said they had the Legion of Decency pledge today."

The Legion of Decency pledge! That was when everybody stood up in church and said, all together, that they wouldn't go to see movies they weren't supposed to see. It would be an even worse sin to see *Gone With the Wind* after taking the pledge. Or would it be two sins? Oh, why did the Legion of Decency pledge have to come along now, just when *Gone With the Wind* was coming to the Lebanon Theater? It wasn't fair!

She wiggled her nose cautiously. It seemed to have

quieted down. She slipped her damp handkerchief back into her purse. Somehow, she had to get out of taking that pledge.

When Mrs. Flynn and Moira entered the church, Moira's eyes moved quickly over the pews. The church was crowded. Good! Maybe she could get into a seat by herself, a seat that didn't have any room for her mother. Then she would just keep quiet and not take the pledge.

The usher was pointing to the front of the church. Ushers always wanted you to go to the front of the church. But Mrs. Flynn shook her head. She marched down the center aisle, her head moving back and forth as she surveyed the pews. Moira followed, her eyes making the same survey.

Then she saw it. A little space on the very end of one pew. "Mom," she said, tapping her mother's back and at the same time sliding into the space. She knelt down, closing her eyes.

When she opened her eyes, Moira couldn't see her mother. She must have knelt down in another pew.

Father Monahan's tall, thin figure appeared on the altar, wearing green vestments. Following him was another priest, shorter and younger, and the altar boy. She had never seen the other priest before, but the boy was familiar. Tom McNeilly from her class.

"In nomine Patris . . ."

The mass was starting. Moira opened her prayer book. Father Monahan galloped through the Latin, while the congregation followed him on the English side of their prayer books. The other priest and Tom McNeilly rushed around the altar, carrying the big book back and forth, handing Father things, and giving answers. Sometimes the altar boys made mistakes, and Father gave them his awful stare. But Tom never made any mistakes.

"Dominus vobiscum," rumbled Father Monahan.

"Et cum spiritu tuo," answered Tom and the other priest.

Father Monahan was stepping forward to give his sermon already. "I know you noticed someone new with me today," he said. "Someone new and considerably younger than myself!"

Laughter rolled briefly through the congregation.

"Father Deschamps has just graduated from the seminary. He'll be helping us out for a while."

Smiling, Father Monahan looked back at Father Deschamps, who was sitting in a chair beside the altar. Father Deschamps smiled and nodded.

"Our sermon today will be based on St. Paul's Epistle to the Thessalonians," said Father Monahan.

Moira covered a yawn with her prayer book. Then she turned to the back of the prayer book. Sometimes you found interesting things back there. A paragraph about St. Frances caught her eye.

At eleven years of age, St. Frances married Lorenzo de Ponziani, with whom she had six children. She was the perfect Christian spouse ...

Eleven years of age! That was the same age she was! What would it be like to be married? She looked up at the stained glass windows, imagining it. A face swam into her mind, a pale face with freckles. Ronald Colligan. Everybody said Frank Hrazak was the best-looking boy in both seventh grades, but she didn't think so. If she had to pick someone, it would be Ronald. Her mouth was so dry!

". . . Legion of Decency pledge," Father Monahan was saying. "Will you please stand?"

This was it! Moira stood up. As she did, she saw a familiar green suit two pews ahead of her and across the aisle. Her mother.

"Repeat after me: 'I do solemnly promise ...' "

The congregation chanted: "I do solemnly promise ..." Moira kept her lips closed. Ahead of her, she could see her mother's lips moving.

" '... to avoid those films which have been judged as serious occasions of sin ...' "

Moira's eyes slid in the other direction. She drew in her breath. The woman next to her was Mrs. Lemay! She was in the Altar Society with her mother! Moira stretched her lips into a feeble smile as her eyes met Mrs. Lemay's eyes.

" '. . . in whole or in part . . .' "

Moira moved her lips but without making any sound. She was careful not to shape them into the words of the pledge. Instead she mouthed the words to a song:

In a cavern, in a canyon,

" 'By the Legion of Decency,' " said Father Monahan.

Excavating for a mine,

" 'As well as those places which show . . .' " the voice on the altar boomed.

Dwelt a miner 'forty-niner . . .

" '. . . such films as a matter of policy.' "

And his daughter, Clementine.

The pledge was over. Moira sank down in her seat. It didn't count, surely, if you moved your lips to the words of a song, not the pledge? She looked at the statue of Mary, who had her own little altar to the left of the main altar. Mary was Moira's favorite person in Heaven. She never seemed to ask for anything

29

or want you to do anything. And she always seemed to understand your problems. If you were close to the statue in church, you could see a faint smile on the plaster lips.

Moira fixed her eyes on the statue. It doesn't count, does it, Mary? she asked the statue.

Mary's face was hard to see from way back here, but as far as Moira could tell, the plaster statue was smiling just the same as always.

After mass, Moira found her mother in the crowd leaving the church. Just ahead of them, she could see Rosemary Randolph and Teresa Sullivan from her class. They were giggling as they dipped their hands in the holy water basin at the front of the church. On her blond hair Rosemary wore a blue hat that matched her blue dress exactly.

Rosemary saw Moira. Her lips shaped a quick hi, but her eyes were already looking away.

"That girl's in your class," said Mrs. Flynn.

Outside, Mrs. Flynn and Moira headed for the curb. Every Sunday, they crossed the street to buy the newspaper at the drugstore. "You never bring any girls home from school," said Mrs. Flynn as they stood at the curb waiting for the light to change. Her eyes met Moira's.

"It's too far," said Moira, turning her head away.

"I thought you would have made some friends there

by now," said Mrs. Flynn, sounding worried. "This is your third year there."

The light switched to green, so Moira didn't have to answer. What was there to say, anyway? They both knew she had to go to St. Teresa's.

In the drugstore, Mrs. Flynn bought the paper while Moira surveyed the magazine rack. The new *Photoplay* movie magazine was in! And on the cover was a picture of Vivien Leigh. She reached for the magazine.

"Another movie magazine?" said her mother. "You just bought one last week."

"That was *Modern Screen*. This is *Photoplay,* my favorite. And it has a picture of Vivien Leigh on the cover. That means there's a story about her inside. Oh, Mom . . ."

Her mother was already opening her purse again.

As they crossed the street, Moira found the story on Vivien Leigh. It was entitled "She Helps Her Countrymen in War-Torn Britain."

"Watch where you're going, Moira," said her mother as Moira stumbled on the curb.

"Mmmm," said Moira, her eyes skimming the story. There were lots of pictures of Vivien Leigh.

They waited at the bus stop in front of the rectory, the big house where the priests lived. Moira studied the pictures: Vivien Leigh giving a cup of tea to a soldier; Vivien Leigh dancing with another soldier; Vivien Leigh at an air base with a crowd of pilots around her. But the best picture showed Vivien Leigh wearing the cutest uniform and talking to a wounded soldier lying in bed.

She was so beautiful!

"The bus, Moira!" said Mrs. Flynn. "Close that magazine and get on."

The Sunrise Hills bus had stopped right in front of them. In her seat, Moira looked through the pictures once again while her mother began reading the newspaper. "Nothing but war news," said Mrs. Flynn. "It's depressing."

Moira looked over at the paper. The front page showed a photograph of tanks.

"Vivien Leigh, she does all this war work in England," said Moira. "Mom, are *we* going to be in the war?"

"Of course not! They have their problems over there, but they're not our problems. There's a whole ocean between us and them!"

"Vivien Leigh gives soldiers tea and dances with them and visits them in the hospital. She has this darling uniform. See?"

But her mother didn't even look at the magazine. "And you remember what President Roosevelt said last year," she said. 'Your boys are not going to be sent into any foreign wars.' So there's not going to be any war for us. This is a European war."

"We read this story in *Young Catholic* about the Chinese and Japanese," said Moira. "They're fighting, too."

"Well, that's not our problem, either."

Mrs. Flynn bent her head over the newspaper. If there wasn't going to be any war, thought Moira, why were her mother's lips so tight? Why did she have that line between her eyes? Her mother was worried, that was for sure.

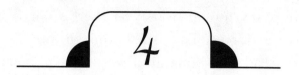

4

The square root of twenty-three hundred and forty-nine," said Sister Gabriel Mary to Moira.

Moira, who was standing at the blackboard, chalked the figures on the board as fast as she could. Sister passed on to the next student standing at the board.

Moira frowned at the numbers she had written. How did you start? Divide off by twos? Yeah, that was it. She chalked a figure tentatively on the board.

"Um-hmm," said Sister, who was on her way back down the line of eight students at the blackboard. Sister's long black draperies made a swishing sound as she walked by. She carried a long pointer.

Moira chalked some more figures. Square roots were so complicated! No, that figure was wrong. She erased it. Next to her, she saw out of the corner of her eye, Mary Lou Prezwalski was just standing there, looking at her number. She hadn't written anything else.

Mary Lou didn't even know how to start. But she was wearing the most darling pink blouse. She had more clothes than anybody except Rosemary Randolph.

"Three minutes," said Sister Gabriel Mary.

Tom McNeilly had already put down his piece of chalk. He was all finished. Tom was such a brain. He could add a whole long list of four-digit numbers in his *head*. Moira chalked some more figures.

There! Her square root was finished, too. It looked okay. Moira put down her piece of chalk.

"Time!" called Sister. She was walking back down the row at the blackboard again, tapping the long pointer on the board as she talked.

"Um-hmm. Good. That doesn't belong there. Carry this over here."

Sister was next to Moira now, chalking in some figures on Mary Lou's number. "Divide off by twos," said Sister. "See? Then you find the largest number that if you square it, will fit into these two on the left. What's that number?"

Six, thought Moira, but Mary Lou just stood there, looking blank.

"Six!" said Sister. "Six times six is . . . what?"

"Um . . . thirty-six."

Sister looked relieved. "Yes! And that's the closest square to forty-one."

"Yes, Sister," said Mary Lou without conviction.

Sister had stopped right next to Moira. "Um-hmmm—good." She swished on.

Moira felt the corners of her mouth turning up. Arithmetic was her least favorite subject, but she was proud when she could do something hard, like a square root.

"Sister, can't we do bigger numbers?" asked Tom McNeilly.

A groan went through the class.

"That's enough!" Sister frowned, raising the pointer. Then she smiled. "I'll give *you* a six-digit number next time, Tom. Row D!"

The eight students in Row D filed up to the board as the eight in Row C filed back to their seats. Moira, behind Mary Lou, watched her wiggle up the aisle to her seat, her pleated skirt twitching back and forth, her shoulders swaying, her blond curls bouncing. Her whole body was in motion. How did she *do* that?

Mary Lou slipped into her seat. Moira dropped into the seat behind her. It was just her luck, she thought, that she had to sit behind Mary Lou this year. She might as well have leprosy, she looked so awful next to Mary Lou.

Sister gave each student in Row D a different problem. "The rest of the class can do this one," she said. She gave another four-digit number, plus a six-digit one for Tom.

Moira opened her notebook. She finished the problem in time to start a drawing of Scarlett at the back of her notebook. Feet scuffled on the floor. Row D was coming back. Bernadette Murphy, passing Moira's desk, looked down. She smiled. Bernadette drew, too. In sixth grade, Bernadette had drawn a picture of St. Teresa on the front blackboard with colored chalk. Sister had liked it so much she kept it on the board for months.

Now Row E, Ronald's row, was filing up to the board. Ronald sat in the first seat, right next to the statue of Mary in the corner. This was a good place for Sister—and Mary—to keep an eye on Ronald. He was first in line at the board.

As Sister gave his number, Ronald's chalk squeaked loudly on the board. Sister winced.

As she was giving the second number, Ronald's chalk squeaked again. Rosemary Randolph, who was next to Ronald, put her hand up to her mouth to hide a smile. Smothered laughter came from the seated students.

"Are you having trouble writing on the board, Ronald?" Sister was walking toward him, tapping the pointer against her hand.

"Sorry, Sister," said Ronald, looking very sincere. "The chalk slipped."

Moira knew that look. All the students did. Nobody could look as sincere as Ronald while he was doing something awful. She wished Jane could see him!

"Well, be careful."

"Yes, Sister."

Turning, Sister walked away.

Squeeeeeeak! Moira winced, then joined the laughter that erupted through the room.

"That's enough!" Sister's pointer swung through the air in a dangerous arc, almost hitting Ronald as it whacked down on the board next to him. Rosemary jumped. The laughter stopped at once.

"Ronald, you can sit down. And stay an hour after school tonight, working on square roots!"

Looking sincere and solemn, Ronald walked back to his seat.

Moira shook with silent laughter. Nobody, nobody could irritate a teacher better than Ronald. He had done it in fifth grade, he had done it in sixth grade, and now he was doing it in seventh grade.

A bell rang.

"Row E, return to your seats. Row A, go to the cloakroom. And class . . ." Sister raised the pointer. "Remember, Father Monahan will be here for catechism class right after lunch. I hope you all studied!" Her glance swept around the room.

A ripple spread through the room. A ripple of uneasiness.

"That's enough!"

When everyone had picked up a tin lunch box or paper bag from the cloakroom, the class lined up, row by row, and marched into the hall. Sister led the way down the stairs. The lunchroom was in the basement. It was the same big hall where they watched religious movies or listened to talks by visiting priests or nuns. At lunchtime, the hall was full of long tables and benches.

The seventh grade was assigned to a group of tables against the far wall. Moira slid onto the end of an empty bench and put her lunch box on the table. The bench soon filled up with other girls. Their conversation flowed over her like something that was happening far away:

"That blouse is so darling, Mary Lou!"

"Somebody in eighth grade told me Sister makes the seventh grade do cube roots later!"

"Isn't he funny?"

"That new priest is so cute!"

Moira opened her lunch box. She didn't talk to anyone and no one talked to her. By now she was used to this strange world where she had to spend so much time until she graduated from eighth grade. Her real world was at the other end of the Sunrise Hills bus route.

Her hands dug into the lunch box. A thermos of hot soup, a peanut butter sandwich wrapped in waxed paper, and two cookies, also wrapped in waxed paper. Below the sandwich was something soft ... Oh no! Another tomato.

This time she wasn't going to eat it.

At the very bottom of the lunch box was the book she had put in this morning. Not *Gone With the Wind*. That would have filled up most of the lunch box, and besides, it weighed a ton. This book, a slim one, had a green paper cover with letters that read, *Father Damien of Molokai*.

She left the book in the box while she drank the soup and gobbled down the sandwich as fast as she could. Then she slid off the bench and made her escape up the steps. She took the book, the tomato, and the cookies out of the lunch box and left the box on the landing. The students picked up their lunch boxes when they came back from the playground.

The big back door swung out onto the playground. She was free!

It was very warm for September. In warm weather, she went to her special place, the place she'd discovered last year. She trotted through the paved upper playground, down the steps, and through the gravel lower playground. This ended in a bank where the older kids sometimes played King-of-the-Mountain. A fence at the bottom separated the playground from the graveyard. She squeezed through a broken part of the fence.

New graveyards were gloomy places, with their wilting flowers and sad-looking visitors. But this graveyard was so old that there were practically no new graves. The letters on most of the gravestones were so worn you couldn't read them. There were no wilting flowers here, no visitors. She liked the old graveyard.

A little way from the fence, she took the road that led up the hill. On the other side of the hill, nobody from school could see you. But you could still see the clock on the church tower. There was a big tree up here, with branches that hung almost to the ground. She stooped under the branches and sank down on the soft ground.

It was so nice here. Behind her was an old stone wall. A little way down the hill, next to the road, was one of those funny little stone houses they had in graveyards. A mausoleum? Something like that. And there was none of the goldenrod or ragweed that made her sneeze anywhere in sight.

She looked at the tomato. Then she raised her arm and threw it at the stone wall. It made a satisfying red splat as it landed. Giggling, she stuffed one of the cookies in her mouth and put the book on her lap. The jacket said *Father Damien of Molokai,* but that was just the jacket. She had taken it off the Father Damien book, which was about a priest who took care of people with leprosy on an island somewhere. After a while he got leprosy himself. Her mother had given her the book for Christmas.

Now she used it to cover her mystery books, because once Sister Seraphim Mary, the principal, had told her mysteries weren't good books. Sister said she should read better books.

Leaning back against the tree, Moira opened the book. It was kind of dark under the tree, but there was enough light to read. She yawned. She was so sleepy . . .

Sitting up with a jerk, she poked her head out from under the branches so she could see the clock on the steeple. Almost one o'clock! Father Monahan's class started in one minute! She leaped to her feet.

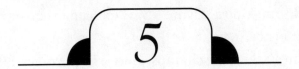

5

Head down, Moira sped along the road toward the school yard. She was running so fast that she almost bumped into the figure coming up the road the other way.

"Oh!" she gasped, taking in the long black cassock, the prayer book, the man's face. It was the new priest! The new priest, and he was saying his office, the prayers priests had to say every day. You weren't supposed to interrupt priests when they were saying their office.

"Oh!" she said again. "I'm sorry!"

The priest put a finger in the prayer book to mark his place. He smiled. "Late?"

"It's almost one! And Father Monahan's giving our class the catechism lesson right after lunch!"

"What's your name?"

"Moira. Moira Flynn." She danced from one foot to the other.

"I'm Father Deschamps. Better run, Moira Flynn!"

She flew off. Through the fence. Up the bank. The playground was deserted. Gravel spurted under her shoes as she ran. She threw open the big back door. There was only one lunch box left on the landing— hers. She grabbed it and stuck the book inside as she tore up the steps.

Heart pounding, she stopped in front of Sister Gabriel Mary's door. She turned the knob very slowly.

Thirty-nine pairs of eyes stared at her from forty seats. Sister, standing against the tall windows, raised her eyebrows until they almost reached the shiny white part of the headdress that came down on her fore- head. She twirled the tassels on the ends of the black cords around her waist. Father Monahan was stand- ing in front of the room, the catechism book in his hand. His bristly gray eyebrows grew together as he frowned.

The statue of Mary in the corner seemed to frown, too. She had never liked that statue, thought Moira.

"Moira Flynn, Father," said Sister. "She's usually on time. Go to your seat, Moira."

The space between the door and her seat looked as wide as the playground. Eyes straight ahead, Moira tiptoed through the wide space to her seat, trying not to make any noise. But her feet seemed to have turned into something huge and heavy.

Clump! Clump! Clump!

"Can anyone name the chief sources of sin?" asked Father.

Mary Lou Prezwalski smiled up at her. It wasn't a nice smile, like the smiles she gave Frank Hrazak. It was a mean smile. I hate you, Mary Lou Prezwalski, Moira thought, sliding at last into her seat. She put her lunch box on the floor and let out her breath.

"Yes, Tom?" said Father to Tom's wildly waving hand.

"The chief sources of sin are seven," said Tom. "Pride, Covetousness, Lust, Anger, Gluttony, Envy, and Sloth, and they are commonly called capital sins." He smiled as if answering questions like that was the most fun in the world.

"What is covetousness, Tom?"

"Covetousness is an excessive desire for worldly things."

Moira opened her notebook to the back pages. She began to work on the picture of Scarlett she'd started that morning. The gown Scarlett wore had a wide skirt. Moira added details as Father walked back and forth, looking at the catechism. His bristly gray hair looked like the fur of a dog that lived on her street, she thought, trying not to smile.

"What is mortal sin?" asked Father.

Bernadette Murphy raised a small hand. She knew almost as many things as Tom did, thought Moira, listening to Bernadette's soft, precise voice. "Mortal sin is a grievous offense against the law of God."

"How many things are necessary to make a sin mortal? Moira?"

Moira dropped her pencil, which rolled off the desk to the floor. It wasn't fair! She was finally in her seat so everybody wasn't looking at her and now they were all looking at her again. She took a deep breath, seeing the three conditions on the page of the catechism. Her words came out in a rush.

"To make a sin mortal three things are necessary: a grievous matter, sufficient reflection, and full consent of the will."

"Good! But there are some long words here, aren't there? What does the catechism say about sufficient reflection?"

Tom waved his hand.

But Father was still looking at her. "Sufficient reflection means that we must know the thought, word, or deed to be sinful at the time we are guilty of it," said Moira, looking at Sister out of the corner of her eye. Sister was smiling slightly.

"I see you've been studying your catechism even if you were late," said Father Monahan. His smile was almost as fierce as his frown. "Now what happens if you commit a mortal sin?"

A forest of hands waved as Father looked away from Moira. Relieved, she retrieved her pencil from the floor.

"Bernadette?"

The soft voice said, "A mortal sin deprives us of spiritual life, which is sanctifying grace, and brings everlasting death and damnation on the soul."

"Um-hmm. 'Everlasting death and damnation.' What does that mean, Bernadette?"

"Hell, Father," said Bernadette in an even softer voice.

"Hell," said Father, pacing all the way to the statue of Mary in the corner next to the windows. "Hell. What is hell?"

Hands waved from all parts of the room, because everybody remembered what hell was. It was hard to forget.

"Kevin?"

"Hell is a state to which the wicked are condemned and in which they are deprived of the sight of God for all eternity, and are in dreadful torments."

Father paced back. "Um-hmm. Dreadful torments! Hell doesn't sound like a pleasant place, does it? But that isn't the worst of it, is it? Eternity! That's the worst of it! For all eternity, we suffer in hell instead of being with God."

Forever. Eternity. Moira bit her lip. It was hard thinking about eternity, it was so long. Was going to see *Gone With the Wind* a mortal sin or just a venial sin? She'd committed lots of venial sins. All you got for penance when you went to confession was a couple of Our Fathers and Hail Marys.

A venial sin wasn't serious. A mortal sin was. You'd probably get this tremendous penance, a few masses at least, for a mortal sin. And if you died before you went to confession . . .

Eternity!

She wanted so much to know if going to see *Gone With the Wind* was a mortal sin, But she couldn't ask Father Monahan—even in private. He was so scary, with those eyebrows and that rumbling voice. And somehow she knew that he would feel that a B movie was something no Catholic should see. It wouldn't make a bit of difference to him that the movie had won ten Academy Awards or that her best friend was going to see it.

At the end of the catechism lesson, Father raised his hand and made a big sign of the cross in the air. *"In nomine Patris . . ."* His blessing. Moira touched her forehead, chest, and shoulders, making the sign of the cross.

The class got to its feet as Father turned to leave the room. At a nod from Sister, they chorused, "Thank you, Father!"

"Father, may I speak with you?" asked Sister.

Father nodded.

"Moira, put your lunch box in the cloakroom," said Sister. "Tom, take the class. I'll be back in a few minutes."

Didn't she miss anything? wondered Moira. She put her lunch box next to a pink one with pictures of movie stars pasted on it. Mary Lou's.

Laughter was coming from the classroom. What was happening?

When Moira came out of the cloakroom, Tom was standing in front of the room. Ronald had turned around in his seat to face the class. Ronald's hair was standing on end so it looked like Father Monahan's, and he had pulled his eyebrows together and screwed up his eyes into little slits. "Dreaaad-ful torments for e-terrrr-nity," he said in Father Monahan's voice.

Nervous laughter rippled through the room.

"C'mon, Ron," said Tom, looking uneasy. He had pulled the geography chart down in front of the blackboard, Moira saw, but nobody was paying any attention to it.

In the front seat, John Klinghammer made a silent signal. Ronald smoothed his hair and folded his hands on his desk.

The door opened, and Sister glided into the room, robes floating behind her. "Thank you, Tom. I see you've pulled down the geography chart."

"Yes, Sister. But everything's changed on the chart on account of the war."

"That's right, Tom." Sister picked up her pointer. "All these countries—France, Belgium, Holland, Poland, Austria, Czechoslovakia, Denmark, Norway . . ." The pointer was sweeping around the big map. "All these belong to Germany now."

"England and the Soviet Union are the only ones left that are fighting Germany," said Tom to the class. "The Soviet Union and Germany, they were allies, but Germany invaded the Soviet Union this summer without any warning. This is the Soviet Union." He pointed to a big place on the map.

As Tom and Sister looked at the map, with their backs to the class, Ronald Colligan made his arms into a rifle. He fired at Tom. Moira smothered a giggle. Tom was always telling the class something.

"We're helping the British with Lend-Lease," said Sister. She made one of her sudden turns to face the class. "Does anybody know what Lend-Lease is?"

Tom started to talk, but Sister saw Ronald's hand. "Ronald?"

"We gave all these ships to England," said Ronald. "And they don't have to pay us till later."

Sister gave Ronald one of her small smiles. "Correct. I'll distribute *Young Catholic* now."

They were still reading *Young Catholic* when the bell rang.

50

"Row D." Sister changed the order in which the rows went to the cloakroom every day, so every row would get a chance to be first. When it was Row C's turn, Moira was surprised to find that Frank Hrazak from Row D was still in the cloakroom. He held the pink lunch box.

"Mary Lou," he whispered, "please go to the party with me."

Moira's heart lurched. She had never heard that tone of pleading in a boy's voice. Would any boy ever talk to her like that?

Mary Lou brushed past Moira, the pleated skirt twitching, the pink shoulders swaying. *"Thank* you," she said, taking the lunch box.

Moira walked slowly out of the cloakroom with her lunch box and book bag, hoping to hear more. But the scuffle of feet of Row C going and Row B coming drowned out everything. She stood by her desk, holding her book bag in one arm, her lunch box in the other.

The bell rang. "Row C," said Sister. The rows took turns leaving, too.

"Moira," said Sister as Moira rushed by. "Would you wait? I'd like to talk to you."

Moira stopped, one foot out in front of her. Inside her stomach, something felt funny.

She stood at the front of the room, next to the list for the kids who were making the First Fridays. Everybody was gone now but Ronald and Sister. And her. Moira's eyes slid down the names on the First Fridays list. Bernadette Murphy. Tom McNeilly. Teresa Sullivan. Nancy Zucker. Only a few more. If you went to mass the first Friday of every month for nine months and took Communion every time, you got a plenary indulgence. That meant you didn't have to suffer for your sins in purgatory after you died. Instead you went straight to Heaven. Moira had never been on the First Fridays list. It was the religious kids who were on it. They were the kids Sister liked.

Moira's nose itched all of a sudden. She pushed her handkerchief against it. Why would Sister want to talk to her?

"Ronald," said Sister, "do the square root of twenty-nine hundred and seventy-six. Moira, let's walk down the hall."

Nose still buried in the handkerchief, Moira followed Sister out of the room. Side by side, they walked down the hall. Sister was tall, thought Moira. Taller than her mother. Almost as tall as her father.

"You left the lunchroom early today, Moira."

Somebody told, thought Moira. Who?

"You leave early every day," continued Sister.

Who told? Mary Lou? But it could have been a whole bunch of girls. None of them liked her. And she didn't like them! A sneeze tore out of her nose before she could stop it.

"Achoo!"

"Where do you go?" asked Sister.

"I . . . take a walk," she mumbled behind the hand-kerchief. Not exactly a lie. Lying was a sin. But she did walk.

They were at the end of the hall. Sister turned and Moira turned with her. They started back.

"Alone?" said Sister.

Moira nodded.

When they reached the door of Sister's room, she stopped. The pale blue eyes looked into Moira's. "I'll see you Monday," said Sister. Her robes swirled as she turned and glided back into the classroom.

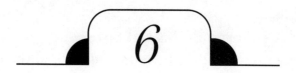

6

The car behind Moira slowed down, then stopped. A horn honked.

"Remember me?"

"Daddy!" Moira climbed into the passenger seat of the Ford, next to her father's big briefcase. He had been gone all week, but now it was Friday evening and he was home.

He leaned over to kiss her head.

"Where'd you go, Daddy?"

"Aliquippa. Beaver. Butler. Zelienople. Universal Uniforms in Aliquippa got an order for five thousand uniforms from the army. So Universal bought fifty of our sewing machines."

"Oh, that's good, Daddy." He would get extra money, a commission, for selling all those machines. "Why does the army want so many uniforms?"

The Ford turned into their driveway. "The new draft has put a million men in the army. That's a lot of men—and they'll need a lot of uniforms. And there'll be more. We're going to get into the war."

"Today in school, we saw all these countries Germany took over, Daddy. Everything but England! And Germany's trying to take over the Soviet Union right now!"

"I'm glad we're getting something for our money at that school." The Ford came to a stop. "I tell you, though, I sure hate to help England. When I think about what England did to Ireland . . ."

Moira opened the door and jumped out before he could say anything more about what England did to Ireland. Mr. Flynn climbed out his side. He walked to the back of the car and raised the trunk lid. His suitcase was in the trunk. He lifted it out.

"I've got something for you," he said. He handed her a paper bag. "Universal had these made up for a sales meeting."

She opened the bag. Inside was a small U.S. flag on a metal base. Printed across the base were the words: AMERICA AND UNIVERSAL: BOTH NO. 1

He had such funny ideas about giving people things! "Thanks, Daddy," she said. Twirling the flag, she followed him into the house. The smell of fried fish hung in the air.

"Ah," said her father. "Catfish!"

They always ate fish on Fridays. It was a mortal sin to eat meat on Fridays. Unless, of course, you weren't a Catholic. If you weren't a Catholic, you got to do a lot of things.

Like see *Gone With the Wind*.

Her mother appeared from the kitchen, the spatula in her hand. "Dave," she said, tilting her head so her cheek faced him. "Good trip?"

He dropped a kiss on the cheek. "Um-hmm. I'll tell you about it at dinner. How're the tomatoes?"

"Lots of them are ripening. I made a tomato salad."

He carried his suitcase upstairs. Moira followed him. In the big bedroom, he set the suitcase on the bed.

"Have you got *Life* magazine, Daddy? And *Look*?"

"Both." He took a pile of magazines and a big book out of the suitcase. "I finished my book on the Irish potato famine. That's a good book, Moira. You ought to read it and find out how the English let a million— a million!—people die in Ireland. Millions of others had to leave for other countries."

"I'm still reading *Gone With the Wind,* Daddy," said Moira quickly. She paged through *Life*.

"That's one of your mother's books. I don't like her books. I like history." He took some shirts out of the suitcase.

"It has lots of history in it, Daddy. About the Civil War. I've read up to the place where Scarlett's in At-

56

lanta and the Yankees are only a hundred miles away, but she has to stay there because Melanie, that's her sister-in-law, is having a baby."

"Mmmmmm. Let me see it after dinner. I don't have any books to read and the library's closed tonight."

"You can't read it now, Daddy!" She shouldn't have talked about *Gone With the Wind.* "I'm reading it. I'm only on page 291!"

"If I like it, I'll go through it fast. You read the book on the potato famine."

"Daddy!" She didn't want to read his book on the potato famine. He was always reading long, boring books about battles and awful things that had happened in Ireland. And most of them had happened such a long, long time ago.

After dinner, she brought *Gone With the Wind* to her father, who was sitting in his chair in the corner of the dining room.

"Thanks, sweetheart." He pulled her close as he opened the book. "Mmmmmm. It's about a woman."

"Scarlett, Daddy. She's so beautiful. All the men are crazy about her."

"Mmmmmm." He turned a page. "Mmmmmm. Mmmmmm." He turned another page. "You go read something else tonight. Tomorrow night you'll get it back." He leaned back in his chair. He put his legs up on the hassock. He turned another page.

"You can't finish it by tomorrow night, Daddy. And I was reading it!" But he didn't even hear her, he was so deep in the book already. Sighing, she ran up the steps to her room. At least she had *Life*. And *Look*.

When Moira got up the next morning, her father was sitting in the same chair in the same position, the big book on his lap. But now almost half of the pages were on the "read" side of the book. He was halfway through!

"Daddy!"

He waved her away.

In the kitchen, her mother was sitting at the breakfast table, drinking coffee.

"Mom, Daddy's halfway through it already!"

"He read it most of the night." She shook her head as she stood up. "You want some cherry coffeecake?"

By lunchtime, there were lots more pages on the "read" side of the book in her father's lap than on the side he hadn't read. Moira stood in the kitchen doorway eating and watching him read and eat at the same time. Bite, turn page. Bite, bite. Swallow coffee. Turn page. He never looked up. If you talked to him, he waved his hand at you.

After lunch, she ran up to her room. Her movie-star paper dolls were in the bottom drawer of her chest. She took out the pile. Each set of dolls had its own cardboard-covered book with a scene from a movie on the front. Inside were pages with the very same costumes the stars had worn in the movie. When you cut out a costume and put it on a doll, it was almost like the star was right there, being the person in the movie.

She picked up the books one by one.

Laurence Olivier and Greer Garson in *Pride and Prejudice*. Ronald Colman and Madeleine Carroll in *The Prisoner of Zenda*. Mickey Rooney and Judy Garland in *Babes in Arms*. Marlene Dietrich and James Stewart in *Destry Rides Again*. Ronald and Madeleine used to be her favorites. Their clothes were so elegant. Long gowns with trains, uniforms with lots of gold medals, high boots, tons of jewels, crowns . . .

But that was before *Gone With the Wind*. As soon as she had seen Vivien Leigh smiling from the counter in the dime store, she knew these paper dolls would be the best.

Gently, she lifted out the brightly colored book. On the front, Vivien—wearing the dress from the barbecue—stood before a big white house with pillars. Tara. Clark was beside her. Leslie wasn't on the cover. She opened the book and found the doll with the pale hair and the little half smile. Yes, Leslie did look like Ronald Colligan!

She put the book with the *Gone With the Wind* paper dolls under her arm. At the front door, she yelled, "Going to Jane's!"

Jane's house was six blocks away, a short ride on her bike. Next door to Jane, some people were carrying furniture into the house. She knocked on the frame of Jane's kitchen screen door.

"Hi!" Jane, barefoot, pushed open the door.

Jane led the way to the side porch, where they both sank down on the floor. "My father bought Linda Darnell and Tyrone Power in *Blood and Sand* for me," announced Jane, holding up a paper-doll book.

"Nobody here has those paper dolls yet!" said Moira.

Jane smiled. "I know. He bought them in New York when he was there on business."

"New York," said Moira. Her father never went to New York. All he went to was little towns. First Jane's parents bought tickets for *Gone With the Wind* and now Jane's father had bought her Linda and Tyrone! How could one person be so lucky?

"Linda has one dress that is practically all ruffles," said Jane, paging through the paper-doll book. "There!"

"It's gorgeous," admitted Moira.

"Let's play with Linda and Tyrone instead of Vivien and Clark," said Jane.

Moira shook her head. The new paper dolls were beautiful, but she could see that they didn't compare to the *Gone With the Wind* paper dolls. Nothing did.

"We're going to do the big ball today, remember?" Moira said. "It was in the previews." Jane hadn't read

Gone With the Wind, because it was too long, but Moira had told her the story as far as she had read.

"Well . . . okay. But I'm going to be Scarlett this time."

Moira felt disappointed. She wanted to be Scarlett. But she *had* been Scarlett last time. "I'll be Rhett," she agreed.

"Scarlett wears black," added Jane, picking up her Scarlett doll and putting on a black dress.

Moira put a black suit with a ruffled white shirt on Rhett.

"You start," said Jane.

"My dear Miss O'Hara," said Moira in a deep voice, walking the Rhett paper doll toward Scarlett, "I hardly hoped you'd recall me."

"Why, it's Captain Butler," cried Jane, moving the Scarlett doll in her black gown.

But somehow, Moira thought as the game went on, paper dolls weren't as much fun today. Jane forgot to have Scarlett say some important things, things Scarlett *had* to say. It was like Jane's mind was on something else. Jane had been like that more and more lately.

Then, just as the Scarlett doll was going to dance with the Rhett doll, Jane looked toward the house next door.

"There's one of them!" she whispered.

Moira looked up. A boy was standing on the front steps of the house.

"There are two—twins!" whispered Jane. "They just moved in next door. They're *sophomores.*"

Jane had dropped the Scarlett doll, Moira realized, dropped it right on the floor. The Scarlett doll's black bonnet had fallen off.

"They're the cutest boys I've ever seen!" whispered Jane.

They didn't go back to playing paper dolls. Instead, thought Moira as she biked home, Jane had spent the whole rest of the afternoon talking about the twins. Not only that, but she insisted they stay in the bathroom for the longest time, because the window overlooked the kitchen next door. Jane had seen a twin getting a glass of water in the kitchen that morning. But the twins didn't come back into the kitchen while they were watching.

Jane hadn't even mentioned Scarlett and Rhett and Ashley and Melanie anymore. Moira shook her head with indignation. It was like they didn't exist, just because two boys had moved next door. Of course some boys were very cute. Ronald Colligan's face suddenly appeared in her mind.

She pedaled faster. But that didn't mean you let the Scarlett doll drop on the floor. That didn't mean you forgot all about the ball where Rhett had paid one hundred and fifty dollars to dance with Scarlett. And to think Jane was going to see *Gone With the Wind* and she wasn't! A wave of indignation flowed over Moira. It wasn't fair!

In the backyard, Moira dropped her bike on the grass. Her father was bending over his tomato plants. At lunch he had been more than halfway through *Gone With the Wind*. When would he be finished so she could read it again?

"Look at this one," he said, holding up a large red ball.

"Uh-huh. Daddy, how much of *Gone With the Wind* do you still have to read?"

"I just finished it."

"You finished it?" Moira stared at her father, unbelieving. Nobody could finish *Gone With the Wind* in one day!

"Finished it," he repeated, searching through the tangle of tomato vines. "Ah!" He held up another large red ball.

"Didn't you think it was a good book, Daddy?"

Her father balanced the two red balls in his hands. "Well, it had a lot of history. And that Gerald O'Hara—"

"Scarlett's father," breathed Moira.

"—he was Irish. Named his place Tara. That's where the Irish kings lived a long time ago."

"Tara," repeated Moira. She hadn't realized it was an Irish place. "Daddy, wasn't it the best book you ever read?"

"Hold these." Handing her the two red balls, he dove into the tomato vines again. He came out with a greenish-red ball. "I'll let this one ripen inside."

"Daddy—"

"What I like is a history book, Moira, not a book with all this made-up stuff in it. But that book had a lot of history and it's better than the ones your mother usually reads, all about murders and detectives."

They walked toward the house carrying the tomatoes. Daddy liked *Gone With the Wind,* thought Moira. Maybe this was the time to talk about the movie again.

"Daddy, we saw the previews for the movie of *Gone With the Wind.* It's coming to the Lebanon Theater next month. Vivien Leigh is Scarlett. She is so beautiful! The movie is just like the book, Daddy. *Lots* of history. Don't you want to see it?"

"What's the name of that woman?"

"Vivien Leigh?" Moira looked up into her father's face, puzzled.

"Vivien Leigh. I saw her in a newsreel. A newsreel about England. She's got an English accent. She's English. You know what the English did to the Irish."

"Oh, Daddy!" Now Daddy would never care about the movie, just because Vivien Leigh was English. It wasn't fair!

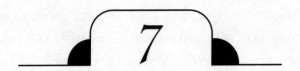

J ohn Klinghammer! St. Vitus."

John Klinghammer's voice began the story of St. Vitus. They were reading selections from *The Lives of the Saints.*

"St. Vitus expelled an evil spirit from the son of the Roman emperor Di ..."

"Diocletian," came Sister's voice as she prowled up the first aisle next to the blackboard.

"Di-o-cle-tian. Members of the emperor's court at ..."

"Attributed." Sister's voice was in back of them now. From the sound of her footsteps, she was stalking toward the windows, following her usual route.

"... at-trib-u-ted St. Vitus's powers to witchcraft because he would not sacrifice to the Roman gods. He was cast into a pot filled with molten lead, but

65

came out without injury. Then he was given to a lion, but the beast crouched before him and licked his feet. Finally he was stretched on a rack, which dislocated his limbs. At this point a great storm arose that destroyed many Roman temples and an angel descended from Heaven to lead St. Vitus home."

Keeping her place in *The Saints* with a left-hand finger, Moira opened her loose-leaf notebook to the last page. She began to draw Scarlet's head as John's voice stumbled on. Scarlett was wearing a bonnet Rhett had given her. She was supposed to dye it black because she was a widow, but Rhett wouldn't let her, so she left it green. The brim was wrong. Moira erased. Yes, that was better. Under the bonnet, Scarlett smiled at Rhett. Moira smiled a Scarlett smile. . . .

A rustle in back of her. She closed the notebook quickly.

"You like to draw, Moira."

Her stomach knew that voice. "Yes, Sister," she said as something inside her stomach curled up tight. Sister hadn't headed toward the windows. She had padded right down their aisle as softly as a cat.

"Come up to my desk." Robes rustling loudly now, Sister moved down the aisle.

Mary Lou turned around to smile her nasty smile as Moira stood up. She walked slowly down the aisle to Sister's big desk. First somebody had told that she was leaving the lunchroom early. And now Sister had caught her drawing. What an awful year this was going to be! Suddenly her nose began to itch. She fished her handkerchief out of her pocket.

Sister was opening her bottom drawer. Last year, in sixth grade, Sister Excelsis Mary had kept a ruler in her bottom drawer. Every Friday, she lined up kids who had been bad that week and hit their hands with the ruler. Moira pulled her arms close to her body. She could still hear those whacks. Ronald Colligan's hand got hit every week.

She couldn't stand it if Sister hit her hand with a ruler.

Sister took a box out of the drawer. She put it on top of the desk. Then she took a cardboard folder out of the same drawer and put that on top of the desk.

"Tom McNeilly!" called Sister. "St. Joseph of Cupertino." In a lower voice, she said to Moira, "I need someone to draw a fall scene on the blackboard." She took a piece of red chalk out of the box. "I have chalk in all different colors here. And fall pictures." She tapped the folder. "Would you like to try it, Moira?"

"At Grotella," read Tom, "seventy occasions are recorded when St. Joseph levitated. Once, when the friars were building a shrine, ten men could not lift a cross that was thirty-six feet high. St. Joseph flew seventy yards to the cross, picked it up as if it were a straw, and put it in its place."

Why was Sister giving her a drawing to do on the

board instead of a punishment? It was the religious kids like Bernadette Murphy who did drawings on the board. Moira's mind whirled. She didn't want to draw on the board while everybody was watching. But she couldn't say no. Drawing on the board while everybody was watching was bad, but having your hand hit with a ruler while everybody was watching was even worse.

"Yes, Sister," she said.

"Sister?" asked Tom's voice.

"Yes, Tom?"

"St. Teresa levitated, too."

"Quite right, Tom," said Sister, opening the folder. "St. Teresa of Avila, for whom our church and school are named, levitated on a number of occasions." She took two pictures out of the folder.

"Sister?" Another voice, John Klinghammer's again. "Sister, how did they do it?"

Sister swung around to fix John with her cold blue stare. "How? Nothing is impossible for God. Remember that." She turned back to Moira. "Look at these pictures, Moira."

Moira stood next to Sister. One picture showed a shock of cornstalks against a moonlit sky. There was an owl sitting in a tree on one side of the picture. The other picture showed a basket of apples and a pumpkin face lit with a candle.

"Which one do you like?" asked Sister.

Moira pointed to the picture of the corn shock.

"I like that one, too." Sister handed the picture to Moira. "I'd like you to put it here." She pointed to the blackboard right in back of her desk, next to the First Fridays list.

Moira had never drawn on anything as big as a blackboard. Setting the picture on the little ledge below the blackboard, she picked up a piece of chalk. Yellow for the corn shock but not bright yellow, because it was night. She would put some brown over the yellow. The moon would be a full orange moon like the kind that hung over the backyard sometimes. The owl couldn't be black, because the board was black. She would make it white.

"Mary Lou Prezwalski! St. Rose of Lima." Sister was prowling the back of the room again.

"When people told her she was beautiful, St. Rose of Lima feared she would be an occasion of sin to someone. She rubbed her face with pepper to disfigure her features with blotches. One day, a woman admired the skin of her hands. St. Rose rubbed them with lime, burning her skin so badly she could not dress herself for a month.

"Ugh!" cried Mary Lou.

"No comments!" cried Sister. "Go on."

It was so weird about St. Rose of Lima, thought

Moira, sketching the shape of the moon. She would have to tell Jane. Jane liked to hear about strange things at St. Teresa's.

"In her last illness," bleated Mary Lou's high voice, "she prayed, 'Lord, increase my sufferings, and with them increase thy love in my heart.' "

Sister had moved to the front of the room, where she stood inspecting Moira's progress. She nodded.

"Can I put a mouse here?" asked Moira, pointing to the bottom of the corn shock.

"A good idea. Bernadette Murphy! St. Zita."

She had never heard of St. Zita, thought Moira. Zita was a nice name, nicer than Moira. Zita Flynn. She drew a small, round mouse in front of the corn shock. Mice were so cute. Her nose had stopped itching! A miracle?

In back of her, Bernadette's small, soft voice was reading almost as if she was enjoying it.

"At the age of twelve, Zita began working as a servant. During a famine, she gave some of her master's stock of food to the poor. One day, the master announced that he was selling his stock of beans that very day because he could get a high price for them. Zita had given most of the beans away. She prayed to Heaven to help her. When the master inspected his beans, none were missing; Heaven had replenished them."

Moira had finished the mouse. She looked up. Sister was smiling her small smile at Bernadette. All the sisters liked Bernadette. Bernadette was good. And smart. She could draw, too. Then Sister pulled the large watch from her pocket.

"It's almost three o'clock," announced Sister. "Moira, put the chalk away; you can finish tomorrow. But don't leave yet. I want to talk to you."

Sister didn't want her to leave. Sister was going to do something awful to her after all. Something in Moira's stomach was curled up tight again as she put the pieces of chalk back into the box.

The bell rang.

Row by row, the class went into the cloakroom. Row by row, they formed into a line at the door. When everyone had disappeared out the door, Sister moved back to the desk, her hands in her long sleeves. She said, "Do you know that the Sisters of the Most Precious Blood in Northvale have a Saturday art school, Moira?"

"No, Sister."

"St. Luke's, it's called. Bernadette Murphy is going this year."

Art school. She'd never thought of going to art school. And with Bernadette, who was so good and smart and popular.

"Ask your parents about it," said Sister. "It's fifty cents a lesson."

"Yes, Sister."

71

"You may go, Moira."

"Yes, Sister. Thank you, Sister!"

Moira walked through the empty hall and out the big front door. There were only a few students left on the wide walk that led up to the street. One of them was Bernadette Murphy, who was talking with Rosemary Randolph. Then Rosemary went up the walk while Bernadette turned toward the church next door. She was going to make a visit, thought Moira. That's what they called it when you went into church for a little while just to say some prayers. Bernadette was always making visits.

As Moira went up the walk, she heard Bernadette call her name.

"Moira!"

Moira stopped. Bernadette came up to her. "Moira! I like your drawing. That mouse is so cute!" Bernadette smiled, two dimples appearing at the corners of her mouth.

Surprised, Moira mumbled, "Thanks."

"I'm going to art school this year at the Sisters of the Most Precious Blood. Maybe you can go, too."

Moira nodded. "Sister told me. I'll ask my parents."

Bernadette walked back to the church as Moira trotted to the bus stop. Art school! And with Bernadette! Moira stood at the bus stop, clasping her books to her chest. Her mother would want her to go to art school. But her father didn't like to spend money on things like school. She would have to plan her strategy carefully.

It wasn't until she was seated on the bus that she remembered. She and Jane always went to the matinee on Saturday.

There was rice and gravy for dinner that night because they had had pot roast yesterday for Sunday dinner.

"I'm drawing a picture of a corn shock and a full moon on the board at school with colored chalk," said Moira, making a well in her rice. She spooned some gravy into it. "It's right in front of the room where everybody can see it."

"Oh, that's nice, Moira," said her mother. "Did Sister Gabriel Mary ask you to do it?"

"Yes, and she likes it. She thinks I should go to art school on Saturday. There's this art school in Northvale run by the Sisters of the Most Precious Blood." She looked at her father.

"Does Sister Gabriel Mary know they raised the tuition at St. Teresa's this year?" asked Mr. Flynn.

"The art class is only fifty cents every Saturday," said Moira, turning to her mother.

"Fifty cents, that's not very much, Dave," said Mrs. Flynn. "But Northvale's so far to go, Moira. You have to take two streetcars. By yourself, too."

"There's this other girl in class, Bernadette, who's going, too."

"Another girl." Her mother nodded, smiling. "You could get to know each other, going to art school. Do you want to go?"

"Yes!" Bernadette's dimpled face appeared in her mind.

"You're getting good commissions now, Dave," said Mrs. Flynn.

Sensing a moment for a shift in tactics, Moira leaned toward her father. "Can I go, Daddy, please?"

"I pay tuition every year because you have to go to a Catholic school, and now you're talking about art school. I never went to art school. Your mother never went to art school."

"Your niece is going to art school, Dave," said Mrs. Flynn with a triumphant smile. "Lovely work she's doing, too, Margaret says. And Nancy's taking piano. Girls do things like that now. Maybe Moira will grow up to be an artist."

Mr. Flynn pushed his chair back from the table. "All right, all right, try it for a few months."

Moira smiled at her mother. Her mother smiled back. Art school! She was going to art school, and with Bernadette. But that meant she couldn't go to the matinee with Jane on Saturday. She had to call Jane.

After dinner, Moira and her mother did the dishes.

The radio played a familiar song, a beautiful song, but without any words.

"'Tara's Theme'!" cried Moira. "The music from *Gone With the Wind*!"

Her mother nodded. "Lovely," she said when it was over. She began to sing the melody.

Her mother had a good voice, thought Moira. She liked to hear her sing. When her mother had finished, Moira said, "Mom, don't you *want* to see the movie?"

"It doesn't matter what I *want* to do. The Church says it's a sin."

She could never tell her mother she was going to see *Gone With the Wind*. She could never tell her after she'd seen it. She would have to keep it a secret forever. The dishes were done. Moira hung the damp dish towel on the back of the door.

In the hall, she picked up the phone and dialed Jane's number. Jane's mother said Jane would call Moira back as soon as she finished her arithmetic homework. When the phone rang a little after eight, Moira rushed down the stairs to grab it.

"I just finished four square roots," said Jane, groaning.

"Square roots are *horrible*," said Moira. "Guess what? I'm going to art school at the Sisters of the Most Precious Blood in Northvale. Daddy said I could. But it's on Saturdays."

"Northvale's a long way," said Jane.

"I know. I can't go to the matinee. It takes too long to get to Northvale and back. I'm sorry!"

Jane received this in silence.

"We could go on Sunday," offered Moira.

"It's not the same movies. And it's more expensive."

"I know. But I really want to go to art school. Jane—maybe I'll be an artist when I grow up!"

"I have to go," said Jane. "I have another square root to do."

There was a click and Jane was gone. Moira climbed slowly back to her room. Jane was mad.

Moira and Bernadette walked up the dark stairs at St. Luke's School of Fine Arts. At the top of the stairs was a life-size painting of an old man who seemed to stare at them with piercing eyes.

"St. Luke," said Bernadette.

"How'd you know?"

"See the ox behind him? That's his symbol. He's the patron saint of artists. And doctors."

Bernadette knew so much about religion, thought Moira as she followed her down a dark hall. The nun downstairs had told them that the room for the seventh and eighth graders was the last one on the right. The door was open.

Inside, the big room was full of long tables, and almost every one of the seats along them was taken by a girl. No boys. This must be a girls' art school.

The windows along the far wall were open. It was warm.

Bernadette surveyed the room quickly. "C'mon," she whispered, nudging Moira.

They slid into two seats at the end of the first row. Bernadette spread her pleated skirt carefully around her.

In front of the room was a nun with a big head-dress. The white part came forward so far around the her face that she could see only in front of her.

Suddenly Moira's nose began to itch. Grabbing her handkerchief, she pressed it hard against her nose. It hadn't itched all the way here, but now it was acting like she was in a field of goldenrod.

The nun was looking at them. "You are . . ." she said.

"Bernadette Murphy, Sister," said Bernadette, standing up.

Moira stood up, the handkerchief still pressed to her nose. She opened her mouth to say her name but a sneeze burst out of her nose instead. *Achoooooooo!*

"God bless you," said the nun, but her words were cut off by another sneeze and then another.

Bernadette answered. "Her name is Moira Flynn, Sister."

Moira sank down in her chair, feeling limp. Her eyes were watering and her nose was dripping. Hold-ing the handkerchief to her nose, she cast a look of gratitude at Bernadette. Bernadette smiled. Bernadette was nice.

The nun, meanwhile, had checked their names off on a piece of paper. Next to her, Moira noticed for the first time, was a tall vase with weeds stuck in it. One of the weeds had yellow flowers on it.

Goldenrod! The thing she was most allergic to! It always made her sneeze and sniffle.

"Welcome to St. Luke's School of Fine Arts, girls," said the nun. "I'm Sister Dymphna. Today we'll draw this vase of wildflowers in pencil. For those who do not have art pencils and paper with them, there is a supply on my desk here. But please buy these items in our art store on the first floor before you leave today."

Still holding the handkerchief to her nose, Moira took a pad of drawing paper, a pencil, and her art-gum eraser out of her cardboard folder. It was just her luck that they had to draw goldenrod, the thing she was most allergic to. Maybe she could hold her handkerchief against her nose with one hand and draw with the other. She spread out her materials.

Bernadette was already sketching. She drew slowly and carefully.

Moira eyed the vase. It was tall. The weeds were tall, too. Besides the goldenrod, there was a spray of something with red berries and a lot of different long grasses. She had to leave room for it all, so it would be a good idea to start the vase halfway down the page. She began to draw.

Oh! She'd wrinkled her paper. That was because she wasn't holding it while she erased. She took the handkerchief away from her nose, held the paper with one hand, and erased.

Achooooo! The sneeze came out so fast she didn't have time to get the handkerchief to her nose. Little damp spots appeared on her paper.

"God bless you," said a voice from in back of the room. Sister Dymphna.

"Are you okay?" whispered Bernadette, her face worried.

"Goldenrod," whispered Moira, nodding her head toward the vase. "I'm allergic." Already, her handkerchief was a small damp ball. She opened her purse and searched through the contents for another handkerchief. But though she found a wadded-up paper from last week's arithmetic test, a candy wrapper, and the green hair clip she thought she'd lost, there wasn't another handkerchief.

Bernadette opened her tiny white purse. Inside, Moira could see, were a rosary, a coin purse, a tiny package that probably contained a veil to wear in church, and a pink handkerchief. That was all. Bernadette held out the handkerchief, which had a flower embroidered on one corner.

She could have hated Bernadette for being so neat,

except that she was so nice, thought Moira, taking the handkerchief. They'd talked about *Gone With the Wind* most of the way down to the art school. Bernadette hadn't read it, so Moira started telling her the story, just the way she did with Jane. Bernadette said it was very exciting.

Moira picked up her pencil again. This time, she got the vase in the right place, but it was lopsided. She erased some more. Her whole paper was full of eraser crumbs. Bernadette, she noticed, didn't seem to erase at all. And she was almost finished with the vase, even though she drew so slowly. It took up only a small part of her paper.

Sister Dymphna was coming down the aisle in back of their seats. "Um-hmm," she said, stopping behind Bernadette's chair. "Pretty."

A sneeze was coming! Moira pressed the handkerchief against her nose but there was no stopping the sneezes today. *Achooooooo! Achoooooooo!*

"God bless you," Sister murmured again. "Do you have a cold?"

"Allergies."

"Ah!" Sister glided on without saying anything about Moira's drawing.

Bernadette's handkerchief was a small damp ball now. Moira patted her nose cautiously.

Sister was back in front of the room. She clapped her hands together. "At two o'clock," she announced, "there is a recess. We will have Kool-Aid and cookies at our seats."

The grape Kool-Aid, Moira's least favorite flavor, came in tiny paper cups. The cookies were oatmeal, her least favorite kind. But there was a napkin. Moira stuck it in her pocket. It would do for a handkerchief. Bernadette gave up her napkin, too.

When Sister clapped her hands again at three-thirty, there were four small damp balls in Moira's pocket. Her eyes felt puffy and her nose was stuffed up. The drawing was done. The vase was so tall it ran off the bottom of the page. The grasses were so long they ran off the top. And the paper was wrinkled. It was a mess! She hated it.

Bernadette's paper wasn't wrinkled at all. A miniature vase of wildflowers floated in the middle of it, neat and precise. She had erased only a few times.

"Let's put up our drawings," said Sister Dymphna, walking to the wall opposite the windows.

The wall was covered with cork. Moira pinned up her drawing hastily. Soon a crooked line of drawings marched across the cork. It was funny the way different people saw the same thing, thought Moira. The vase didn't look the same in any of the drawings.

Sister was walking down the line of drawings. She used only a word or two to comment on them.

"Neat," she said of Bernadette's.

"Good line," she said of Moira's. "Strong."

Good line? Strong? Moira stared at her messy drawing. From her seat, you couldn't see the wrinkles. Maybe it wasn't so bad.

After the class was over, they waited for the streetcar across from the school. Moira tried to breathe through her nose. But it was too stuffed up. She propped her mouth open a little with her tongue.

A streetcar glided up to them like a nun. The double doors opened.

They sat down in a double seat. "What happens to Scarlett after she gets back to Tara?" asked Bernadette, arranging her skirt around her. That was why Bernadette's skirts never got wrinkled, thought Moira. But who could remember?

"Well, her mother is dead . . ." she said.

"Oh, no!"

"Yes. And her father is crazy."

"Oh, no!"

"Yes. And they're very, very poor and they all have to work very, very hard. Scarlett is in charge and she worries all the time."

By the time the second streetcar was near Lebanon, Scarlett was back in Atlanta, planning to borrow the tax money from Rhett Butler. "That's as far as I read," said Moira.

"It's a lovely story," said Bernadette. "I like Melanie better than Scarlett, though. Scarlett isn't nice."

Moira frowned. Scarlett wasn't really nice. She did

mean things sometimes. But she was so strong, so brave, so beautiful! Maybe a person like that didn't have to be nice, too, the way girls and women were supposed to be. But of course she couldn't say that to Bernadette. Bernadette was so nice herself, much nicer than she, Moira, could ever be.

"You know the movie's coming to the Lebanon Theater," said Bernadette. "My mother won't let me see it, of course." She gave a small sigh.

Moira felt surprised. Maybe Bernadette did want to see the movie, even though she was so religious. "My mother won't let me see it, either," said Moira. "My friend Jane's going with her parents. But they're not Catholic."

They looked at each other, nodding. "Well, it's all right for *them*," said Bernadette.

What would Bernadette say if she knew the person she was sitting next to, a *Catholic*, was planning to go? Bernadette's face appeared in Moira's mind, wearing a shocked look. Moira looked out the window of the streetcar. She could never tell Bernadette, either.

"It's funny," said Bernadette. "You don't—" She stopped.

"What?"

"I probably shouldn't say anything." They were passing a big Catholic church. Bernadette made the sign of the cross.

Moira hastily made the sign, too, though she wouldn't have done it if she were by herself. "Tell me what you were going to say, *please*," she said.

Bernadette looked down at her lap. "Well, they all say you're stuck up."

She didn't ask who said it. She knew. And it was so unfair! "I'm not!" she cried, so loudly that the man in front of them looked around. "I'm not stuck up," she said in a lower voice.

Bernadette's brown eyes looked into Moira's. "They all say that, but you don't seem stuck up, you really don't."

"I'm not!"

"Then why don't you talk to anybody in the class?"

"They don't talk to me!"

"Well, they say you just go right past them with your nose in the air and don't even look at them."

The unfairness of it! There were tears in Moira's eyes, and it had nothing to do with her allergies this time. She remembered those first awful days at school. In the playground, she had gone up to some of the girls in her class but they were talking so fast they didn't even look at her. It was like she was invisible or something. Then they had walked away and she had been left standing there all by herself. The same thing happened next time.

After that she didn't even try going up to them anymore.

But she couldn't say all that, she thought, looking at Bernadette out of the corner of her eye. Bernadette seemed nice, but . . .

"It's hard," said Moira, struggling to find words that would say something but that wouldn't say too much. "It's hard to . . . go up to them. They all know each other and they're talking. I don't know anybody."

"Well, you know me," said Bernadette. "So you can come up and talk to me."

Moira looked out the window again. Today, Saturday, Bernadette was her friend. But what would she do on Monday? Last year, Rosemary Randolph had had this fight with her friends, so she came over and started talking to Moira. But then Rosemary made up with her friends and she didn't talk to Moira anymore.

The streetcar was gliding up to their stop.

"See you Monday," said Bernadette as they stood on the corner. "Okay?" She smiled just a little, showing a dimple.

Swallowing, Moira looked at Bernadette. "Okay," she said.

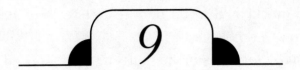
So what was this art school like?" asked Jane.

Jane and Moira were sitting on the floor of Jane's porch on Sunday afternoon. When Moira had called Jane again on Saturday night, Jane had asked her to come over Sunday. Maybe Jane wasn't mad anymore.

"Well, I sneezed practically the whole time," said Moira. "Because we had to draw a vase with goldenrod in it. But Sister said my drawing was strong."

Moira paused. She hadn't mentioned Bernadette yet. "I went with this girl from my class. Bernadette. She's nice. She said to come and talk to her in the playground on Monday."

Jane's brown eyes stared into Moira's. Then, looking away, Jane said, "Maybe you'll be friends."

"Maybe," said Moira. "Not like us, I mean," she

added quickly. "But it'd be nice to have somebody to talk to at school."

Jane's face seem to soften. She smiled and nodded.

Relieved, Moira decided to ask Jane's advice. "But will she remember she said that on Monday? When all her friends are there?"

"Of course!"

Jane never seemed to worry about things like that. If somebody didn't talk to her, she just talked to somebody else. But she and Jane were different. Moira opened her *Gone With the Wind* paper-doll book. "The only thing is, Bernadette is so religious. She blesses herself every time she goes by a Catholic church. And she's always making visits. That's when you go to church when there's nothing going on."

Jane shook her head. "What's the use of going there if there's nothing going on?"

Jane didn't really understand about the Catholic Church, thought Moira. She opened her mouth to tell Jane that God was right up there at the altar whether there was anything going on or not. You could tell he was there by the red light burning in front of the altar. But Jane would just shake her head again if she heard that. In Jane's church, there wasn't even an altar. Moira closed her mouth.

Jane leaned forward. "Listen, I have something to tell you."

"What?" Moira, sifting through paper-doll clothes, pulled out Scarlett's everyday dress. It was Moira's least favorite, but today they were doing the part where the Yankees burn Atlanta. Scarlett couldn't wear anything good if Atlanta was being burned and she had to escape in the wagon.

"One of the twins *talked* to me!"

"What'd he say?"

"Well, he came out on his front porch and he saw me, he looked right at me, and he said, 'Hi!' "

It wasn't exactly talking, thought Moira, walking the Scarlett doll across the porch floor toward Jane. "Well, what did you say?"

"I said, 'Hi.' And then he went back inside." Jane sighed. "Do you think I should have said something else?"

"I don't know. Maybe." It was hard to know what to say to boys. Boys were so *different*. Of course if you were really pretty, like Mary Lou Prezwalski, you never had to worry about saying things to boys. They were always saying things to you.

"I saw the twins together Friday when I was coming home from school," said Jane. "They are *so* cute. I think one is a little bit cuter than the other. His nose is nicer. And his hair."

The Scarlett doll was standing right in front of Jane, but Jane didn't seem to notice. "We're doing the part where they burn Atlanta, and Scarlett escapes in the wagon with Rhett," prompted Moira. "It's my turn to be Scarlett."

"Okay." Jane picked up the Rhett doll, but she didn't look at it. She was looking at the house next door.

Moira made the Scarlett doll walk up to the Rhett doll. "I'm going home to Tara. Oh, Rhett, we must hurry!"

Jane put her hand on Moira's arm. "I would just do anything if one of them would smile at me!" She rolled her eyes upward. "Listen, come upstairs. I've been trying this new thing with my hair."

"But Scarlett . . . and Rhett . . . the fire!"

"We can do that later. C'mon!"

Moira followed Jane up the stairs to her bedroom. The Linda and Tyrone paper-doll book was lying on Jane's dresser. Moira opened it. Jane still hadn't cut out all the costumes. Jane used to cut out every costume as soon as she brought a new paper-doll book home from the dime store. Jane had changed since the twins moved next door.

No, it had started earlier than that. It had started last summer when they went to the swimming pool. Jane spent so much time just looking at boys.

Jane had seated herself on the pink stool in front of her pink-skirted dressing table. She peered into the mirror. Then she grabbed the hair on top of her head and put it into one of the new pompadours. It rose up from her head like a wave.

"Bobby pins," said Jane, taking one. She pinned the pompadour in place.

Next she picked up the hair from one side of her face and put it up on top, too, behind the pompadour. She did the same with the hair on the other side. More bobby pins fastened the sides in place.

"Do you think it makes me look older this way?" asked Jane.

Moira looked at Jane's reflection in the mirror. "Yeeeees," she said slowly. "It does. Vivien Leigh wears her hair that way sometimes."

"Linda Darnell wears her hair this way, too. And Carole Lombard and Ginger Rogers and Betty Grable. Look!" Jane held up a copy of last month's *Photoplay*. Linda Darnell was on the cover, wearing her hair up on the sides and a pompadour on top.

Jane picked up a hand mirror and inspected the back of her hair in it. Then she put down the mirror and looked at Moira. "I've started," she said.

"Started what?"

"You know."

Moira felt bewildered. "I don't! What is this, a mystery?"

"I keep forgetting you're so much younger than I am."

"I'm not! I'm only five and a half months younger!"

"Well, I've been twelve since July, and you'll be eleven until December." Jane's face was solemn as she leaned forward and whispered, "I've started menstruating."

"Oh!" For a moment, Moira couldn't remember what the word meant. Then she heard her mother's voice explaining last spring. Blood. Every month. Pads. It had something to do with babies, and the whole thing, she remembered, seemed very messy.

"You've started?" she said.

Jane nodded. "Last week."

"Do you have to wear those . . . things?"

"Of course!" Spinning around on her stool, Jane inspected herself in the mirror again.

Moira stared into the mirror over Jane's head. Suddenly Jane, her best friend, seemed so different from her. It was like something very mysterious and very important had happened to Jane, something that had changed her forever. She looked the same, at least when she wasn't wearing her hair like a movie star's, but she was different inside.

"I'm going to wear my hair this way from now on," said Jane. "It definitely makes me look older. Do you know the twins are fifteen? Their mother told my mother. Why don't you let me put your hair up?"

When the sides and front of her hair were anchored on top of her head with bobby pins, Moira wasn't sure she liked the way it looked. Her face looked different but maybe not better. "I don't know. . . ." she said.

"Wear it home that way," said Jane. "You can keep the bobby pins. Let's try my new lipstick."

By the time they had each tried the new dark red lipstick, which Jane said was the kind Carole Lombard and Linda Darnell and Ginger Rogers and Betty Grable all wore, it was time for Moira to go home. They had never gotten back to the paper dolls. In front of Jane's house, Moira put the paper-doll book in her bike basket.

"I'm sorry about the matinees—really!" said Moira.

Jane shrugged. "Sally and I are going. We're going to go every Saturday."

Sally lived at the end of Jane's block. Jane called her Silly Sally sometimes.

"Sil—I mean, Sally? I didn't think you liked . . ."

"Sally's going to see *Gone With the Wind* with her parents on Saturday night," said Jane. "That's the same time we're going. Afterward, we're all going to Robinson's for sodas."

Moira took a deep breath. Silly Sally and Jane going to the matinees together was bad enough. But Sally and Jane seeing *Gone With the Wind* together—that was worse. And having sodas afterward. Moira would have to go see the movie all by herself. And come home afterward all by herself.

Just then the door of the house next door opened. A tall boy with dark hair came out. He carried a basketball.

Jane raised her hand, but without looking in their direction, the boy loped down the front walk to the driveway. Halfway there, he threw the ball toward a hoop placed above the garage door. The ball missed.

"He *is* cute," whispered Moira, trying to be polite, but thinking privately that the boy was cute enough, but not nearly as cute as some other boys. Ronald Colligan, for instance.

"I don't know which one it is," whispered Jane. "I can't see his nose."

Moira got on her bike. A few houses away, she turned, lifting her hand to wave. But Jane wasn't looking her way. She was still looking toward the boy in the driveway.

Moira dropped her hand. Jane *was* still mad—a little. But Jane just wasn't the same as she used to be. Maybe when that mysterious and important and messy thing happened to Moira, everything would be all right between them again. Maybe she and Jane would be like they were before.

But in her mind, she saw Jane standing in the front yard, looking the other way.

When Moira got home, her mother was standing at the stove, stirring something in a pot.

"Jane's started," said Moira.

"Started? You mean . . ."

Moira nodded.

"Well, Jane's older than you," said Mrs. Flynn.

"Only five and a half months," said Moira. "Mom, does every girl, every woman . . ."

"Of course," said Mrs. Flynn. "Until they get too old."

"Even nuns?"

"Nuns are women, aren't they? What did you do to your hair?"

"Jane did it. She's going to wear her hair like this."

"I don't like it on you. The lipstick, either. You need a softer color if you're going to wear lipstick. Besides, you know what Sister Seraphim Mary said."

"No lipstick in school," said Moira. Did Sister Seraphim Mary . . . ? It was hard to believe.

In her room, Moira sat on the bed with her paper-doll book. She opened the cover. Scarlett was still wearing the plain dress she wore for the ride in the wagon. When she kissed Ashley in the previews, she wore a dress like that.

She picked up the Ashley doll in one hand and the Scarlett doll in the plain dress in the other. She moved the two dolls together, then apart.

"You do love me! Say it!" she said in Scarlett's voice.

"All right, I'll say it," said her Ashley voice. "I love you."

She closed her eyes, seeing the real, bigger-than-life figures on the screen kissing. She liked Ashley so much better than Rhett. And to think he and Scarlett and Rhett and Melanie would all be appearing in the Lebanon Theater in less than two weeks! If she was going, she had to make her plans. She leaped to her feet.

At the end of her bed was a bookcase. She pulled out *The Green Fairy Book*. Inside were two dollar bills. One was all wrinkled and limp, like an old sheet. The other was stiff and smooth. She pulled out the stiff, smooth dollar and ran her fingers over the surface. Her father had given her this dollar on her last birthday. She could buy a general-admission ticket with it. But she'd have to get it soon or they'd be all sold out.

She put the stiff, smooth dollar back between the pages and stood up. If only she knew whether seeing *Gone With the Wind* would be a mortal or a venial sin. If seeing it was a mortal sin and she died before she got to confession, she would go to hell for eternity. Eternity was so long! Why did Catholics have to worry about things like eternity when Unitarians like Jane didn't? It wasn't fair!

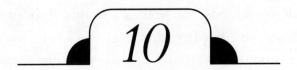

10

What if Bernadette wasn't there?

Slowly, Moira rounded the corner of the school, her handkerchief in her hand. She had been sneezing all morning. The girls from her class, she knew, had staked out the far side of the upper playground as their place this year. They stood there talking in small groups except when they all got together to play games.

There they were. And there, right in the middle of a group of five girls, was Bernadette. Moira swallowed. Her feet seemed to have become large and heavy. Her nose itched. Handkerchief to her nose, she clumped slowly toward the group. Bernadette had probably forgotten what she said on Saturday. Or maybe she hadn't forgotten, but now that she was with all her friends, she wouldn't want to talk to somebody who wasn't a friend.

She wouldn't want to talk to somebody who belonged to a whole different world.

Moira stopped. Rosemary Randolph was one of the girls in Bernadette's group! Rosemary Randolph, who had stopped talking to Moira when she made up with her friends!

But Bernadette was leaning forward, waving. "Moira! Come over here!"

Moira's feet seemed to have lightened magically. She flew over the playground. Besides Rosemary, Nancy Zucker, Jean Winters, and Teresa Sullivan were in the group. Bernadette held a little bouquet of flowers.

"Moira is actually reading *Gone With the Wind*!" cried Bernadette.

The girls all talked at once.

"Are you?"

"I started it but it's so *long*."

"And so *heavy*. It must weigh ten pounds."

"Do you like it?" asked Rosemary.

Moira nodded. "It's the best book I've ever read."

"The movie's coming to the Lebanon Theater October fifteenth," said Bernadette. "Of course I can't go."

"Me either."

"Huh-uh."

"My mother would never let me see a B," said Rosemary. "But my cousin, she's fourteen, she saw it."

"Is she a Catholic?"

"Did her parents *let* her?"

"They're Catholics, but there's just her mother," said Rosemary, "They're divorced and . . ."

"Oh, *divorced.* Well . . ."

Everyone but Moira nodded their heads. Divorced Catholics, the nods seemed to say, might let their child do practically anything. What would the girls think, wondered Moira, if they knew *she* was planning to see *Gone With the Wind?* She couldn't tell any of them, either. The only one she could tell was Jane.

The bell rang. Moira walked beside Bernadette into the school. For the first time since coming to St. Teresa's, she realized, she felt almost like she belonged there.

Bernadette nudged her arm. "You want to sit with us at lunch?" she asked.

"Yes!" Her nose had stopped itching.

As soon as they were in the classroom, Bernadette took her bouquet to Sister. Sister, with a slightly bigger version of her small smile, walked beside Bernadette to Mary's statue. Bernadette took some wilted flowers out of the little vase in front of Mary and replaced them with her own. Bernadette was always doing things like that, thought Moira, pushing her books into the space under her desk. No wonder all the Sisters were crazy about her.

At lunch, Moira didn't say much, just let the talk roll around her as usual. The difference was, she was in the middle of the group, and every once in a while, somebody said something to her or she said something to somebody. It was like she was supposed to be here, like she was part of this world.

"Anybody want this egg?" Rosemary made a gagging sound as she held up a hard-boiled egg from her lunch box.

There were *no*'s all around and an *ugh* from Teresa. Rosemary turned suddenly and stuck the egg in Moira's lunch box. Moira stuck it in Bernadette's. Bernadette stuck it in Jean's. They were all laughing, and by the time the egg got back to Rosemary, the shell was cracked.

"Sister Excelsis Mary sees us," hissed Teresa. "You know how she is about wasted food."

"She keeps telling us about those children starving in the Chinese missions," hissed Nancy.

"Do I have to *eat* this?" mumbled Rosemary, holding out the cracked egg.

"Sister Gabriel Mary caught me throwing out a tomato, so I can't do it anymore," said Moira. "I'll take the egg if you'll take my tomato."

Smiling, they made the exchange.

When they got back to the classroom after lunch,

Sister Gabriel Mary wasn't there. With a scuffling of shoes and creaking of desks, the forty students sat down. If Sister had been there, it would have been quiet, but now everyone seemed to be talking at once.

Sudden quiet. A figure had appeared in the open door. Not Sister Gabriel Mary. Sister Seraphim Mary, the principal. The students scrambled to their feet.

"Good morning, students."

"Good morning, Sister."

"Sister Gabriel Mary will be a few minutes late, class. She asked Tom McNeilly to start the class on *The Lives of the Saints*. Tom?"

"Yes, Sister." Tom walked forward, *The Lives of the Saints* in his hand, as the door closed behind Sister Seraphim Mary. Moira opened her *Saints* with her left hand and her notebook with the other. It was a good time to draw.

"St. Vitus," cried Ronald Colligan before Tom could say a word. "St. Vitus," he pretended to read, "was fried in a skillet with onions and tomatoes, but he said it felt good. Then they boiled him with the spaghetti and he said the water was a little cold."

"C'mon, Ron," said Tom.

Everyone but Tom was laughing. Moira shook with laughter as she picked up her pencil. It was broken. She stood up and headed for the pencil sharpener next to the door. Her drawing was still on the board. It looked good.

"... put a leash on the lion and took him for a walk. St. Vitus is the patron saint of spaghetti and lions."

"Cut it out, Ron!" said Tom's voice above the laughter.

Ronald leaped up. "That's enough!" he said, advancing to the front of the room. He grabbed Sister's pointer from the desk. "The next person who laughs will be run through with this pointer!" He held out the pointer like Ronald Colman held out the sword in *The Prisoner of Zenda*.

More laughter.

Was the knob on the closed door next to the pencil sharpener turning? Yes, ever so slowly! "Sister!" hissed Moira.

But the laughter drowned out her words. "Sister!" cried Moira.

Dropping the pointer on Sister's desk, Ronald dashed to his seat just as the door burst open. Sister Gabriel Mary seemed to spring into the room, her eyes taking in the whole scene at a glance. Her swirling black robes brushed Moira as she passed. Moira shrank back against the wall.

"*What* is going on here?" demanded Sister. "I could hear laughter all the way down the hall! Is this *The Jack Benny Program*? *The Fred Allen Show*?" She pounced on the pointer and whacked it against the wood surface.

Moira jumped.

Pointer in hand, Sister stalked back and forth in front of the class. She turned her head to direct an ice-blue stare at Moira. "Moira! Moira, was that you who said 'Sister'?"

Moira nodded dumbly.

"Return to your seat. I'll talk to you later."

Moira sped down the aisle, the thing in her stomach beginning to curl.

"Ronald! Ronald, it was you who was giving that ... parody of St. Vitus!" said Sister's voice.

Moira sank into her seat and stared toward the awful scene in the front of the room. "St. Vitus, a holy saint in Heaven," Sister was saying, directing the pointer toward the ceiling. "And you were also imitating ... *me!* I heard you, outside the door." She raised the pointer. Moira screwed her eyes closed. Whump! The pointer had come down on something softer than wood or slate.

The forty pupils of Sister Gabriel Mary's seventh grade were so silent it was like nobody was in the room. Moira opened her eyes a tiny slit. Sister and Ronald were staring at each other, frozen, like they were in a photograph in *Life* magazine. The pointer dangled from Sister's hand. Everyone else in the room was staring at Sister and Ronald. Even the statue of Mary seemed to be looking at them.

In the silence, a fly buzzed loudly.

The photograph began to move as Sister walked back to her desk. Ronald moved his hand slowly up to touch his shoulder. Then he dropped his hand back to the desk.

She had hit his shoulder, thought Moira. Sister had hit Ronald with the pointer. A pointer was bigger than a ruler, so it must have hurt a lot. But Ronald's pale face looked just the same. Only his hand touching his shoulder showed that it must hurt. Brave. Ronald was brave. She wasn't brave. What would Sister do to *her?*

"Ronald, Moira, you will remain here after school," said Sister. "Class, open your Bible history."

After school! She had never been asked to stay after school for doing something wrong! The thing in her stomach curled up into a ball. This day, which had started out so well, was turning into a bad day, a very bad day, maybe the worst day of her life.

After the three o'clock bell, the other students tramped out of the classroom with their lunch boxes and books. Bernadette turned at the door to give her a sympathetic look. Then there was silence again in the room. Outside, the faint sounds of the kids going home floated in through the open windows.

What would Sister do? What would she say?

Sister sat at her desk. She was writing, dipping her pen in an inkwell from time to time. Finally she set the pen in the little stand next to the inkwell. She stood up. Pointer in one hand, she glided across the room.

Sister's voice was almost mellow as she spoke. "Learning is not easy, children. Learning is not fun. It is not meant to be enjoyable. No, learning ... is ... work! Hard work!"

Moira dropped her chin into her hands. She liked some of the things they studied. But Sister made it all seem so awful.

Sister had turned and was gliding back. "And what does learning require, Ronald?" The pointer leaped in Ronald's direction.

"Um, studying?"

"Studying, yes, but what underlies all studying, all learning? Moira?" The pointer swung in her direction.

What was the right answer? It wasn't in the catechism. It wasn't in any of the books. It wasn't fair, asking a question that wasn't in any of the books!

"Discipline," barked Sister, withdrawing the pointer. "Discipline! Discipline enables us to persist in a difficult or unpleasant task. Discipline is the key to a Catholic education. Children! Your duty as Catholic children is to learn. God has put you here to do that. And to learn—you must have ..."

The pointer swung in Moira's direction again.

"Discipline," gasped Moira.

"Mmmmmm," said Sister, gliding again across the classroom. "And does a disciplined person amuse the class—the class which is supposed to be *learning*—when the teacher leaves the room?" She stared at Ronald, who shook his head. "And does a disciplined person *laugh* at the antics of such a person? *Help* that person?" The icy blue eyes were looking at Moira now.

Moira shook her head, her whole face hot with embarrassment. That was her, the person who laughed. A person who had no discipline.

Sister was gliding toward the windows again, her feet not seeming to move beneath her long robes. How did she do that? It was like she had on ice skates instead of shoes.

"There are schools, public schools"—and here Sister's eyebrows climbed up almost to the shiny white of her headdress—"public schools that do not stress discipline. Things go on in the public schools ..." Sister's eyes closed for a moment, as if the things that happened in public schools were so awful she couldn't bear to think of them. "A boy or girl who cannot accept the discipline of a Catholic education must go to a public school. There is no place for that boy or girl in a Catholic educational institution!"

Jane liked public school. But maybe Sister had never been in a public school.

Sister was glaring at Ronald. "Do you understand me, Ronald?"

"Yes, Sister." Ronald's face was solemn.

Moira drew in her breath. Was Sister going to expel Ronald?

"Ronald, you will write me a composition on the role of discipline in the life of Our Holy Father, Pope Pius XII. A thousand words. Moira, you will write me a composition on the role of discipline in the life of St. Teresa of Avila, for whom St. Teresa's Church and School are named. Five hundred words. I want these by next Monday."

Sister sat down behind her big desk. "Your bus is due in five minutes, Moira. Hurry. Ronald may go, too."

Silently, Moira and Ronald walked out of the classroom. She had never walked beside him before, thought Moira. It made her feel a little dizzy, the way she'd felt when she had the flu last year. She wished she could think of something to say. But boys were so different, you never knew what to say to them. The silence persisted as they went out the big double doors and down the stone steps.

As they went up the wide walkway, Moira willed herself to turn her head toward him. "Does . . . does your shoulder hurt?"

"Nah!" said Ronald quickly, one hand touching the shoulder and then dropping to his side. "Listen, if you want to tell somebody somebody's coming, you've got to do it *qui-et-ly.*" His voice sank to a whisper on the last word.

She nodded. His eyes were pale blue or gray, like Ashley's in the movie.

They had almost reached the street. Way down the street, she could see the bus coming. It was the bus that came after the one she usually took. How did Sister know she took the bus? Sister must have looked up her bus in a schedule. But why would Sister do that?

"My bus is coming," she said as the bus lumbered toward them.

"You live in the Hills," he said.

She nodded again. Like Sister, he knew something about her. Something she didn't know they knew.

After she got on the bus, she looked through the window. Ronald was walking along the sidewalk next to the bus. He waved a hand. She waved back. Yes, he definitely looked like Ashley, the one she liked so much better than Rhett.

11

"Do you think Father Deschamps will be easier than Father Monahan?" asked Teresa. The bell ending lunch recess had just rung and the students were waiting in line outside the back door to St. Teresa's School.

"I hope so," said Bernadette. "I didn't study enough last night. What are the seven spiritual works of mercy?"

"Admonish the sinner," began Nancy.

The others took it up like the chorus of a song.

"Instruct the ignorant.

"Advise the perplexed.

"Comfort the unhappy.

"Bear wrongs patiently.

"Forgive all injuries . . ."

The voices stopped. "What's the last one?" asked Bernadette. "That's the one I always forget!"

"Pray for the living and dead," said Moira.

"Oh, yeah," said several voices.

"Rita Semina in the other seventh grade says Father Deschamps asked these strange questions in catechism class yesterday," said Rosemary.

"Strange how?" asked Nancy.

"Just strange. They're not in the catechism."

Not in the catechism! Moira looked at the others and saw the same expression on every face. Not in the catechism! If it wasn't in the catechism, how could you study for it?

"It's not fair," said Moira, and everyone nodded.

A bell rang. The students filed into the building two by two, the eighth graders in the lead. Sister Gabriel Mary was standing by the door of her classroom, her hands inside her full black sleeves. Inside the classroom, Father Deschamps stood in Sister's usual place. He wore his long black cassock.

When every student was standing by his or her seat, Sister came inside. She nodded.

"Good afternoon, Father," chorused the group. "Good afternoon, Sister."

"Good afternoon, boys and girls," said Father. "Please be seated."

Seats squeaked and groaned as the class slid into their seats.

Father stood next to Mary's statue. He held an open catechism in one hand. "Let's talk about something very important in the Catholic religion, the divine virtues. Can anyone tell me what those divine virtues are?"

Hands went up. Easy, thought Moira. There were only three.

Father Deschamps pointed to Teresa Sullivan.

"Those graces or gifts of God by which we believe in Him, and hope in Him and love Him, are called the divine virtues of Faith, Hope, and Charity," said Teresa.

"Correct." Father closed the catechism. "And which of those three did St. Paul call the greatest virtue? This isn't in the catechism."

He was doing it! Asking questions that weren't in the catechism. It wasn't fair!

No hands went up. Even the statue of Mary seemed to look a little confused.

"I'll give you a hint," said Father Deschamps. "The answer is in an epistle, a very famous epistle written by St. Paul."

Suddenly the words appeared in Moira's mind. She'd heard them read on the altar last winter. And the winter before that. And the winter before that. "So there abide Faith, Hope, and Charity," she thought, "these three; but the greatest of these is Charity."

"Moira Flynn, you seem to know the answer."

She must have moved her lips! " 'So there abide

Faith, Hope, and Charity, these three; but the greatest of these is Charity.' "

"Correct," said Father Deschamps.

Moira felt a little glow inside. She was the only one who remembered the words from the epistle.

"Charity," said Father Deschamps. "What does St. Paul mean by Charity?"

Tom's hand was waving as usual.

"Tom?"

"Charity is a divine virtue by which we love God above all things for His own sake and our neighbor as ourselves for the love of God."

"In simple terms," said Father, "St. Paul meant love, didn't he? So then we have to ask, what did he mean by love? The love of a man for a woman?"

Frank Hrazak turned his head toward Mary Lou a little and smiled.

"Or the love of a parent for a child?" asked Father Deschamps, looking around the room. But nobody's hand went up, because this wasn't in the catechism, either.

"No, St. Paul didn't mean that kind of love," he said. "The love he was talking about here is the same kind of love Our Lord was talking about when He said 'Love thy neighbor as thyself.' St. Paul and Our Lord meant treating everybody the way you'd like to be treated yourself."

After that Father talked about the Good Samaritan and a lot of other things about love. He never opened his catechism again. It wasn't fair, thought Moira. But it was kind of nice, what Father said. Treating everybody the way you wanted to be treated yourself.

At the end, Father Deschamps asked, "Does anybody have any questions?"

Lots of hands waved.

I could ask him, thought Moira, leaning forward. I could ask him whether it's a mortal sin or a venial sin to see *Gone With the Wind.* He wouldn't give me that awful look, like Father Monahan. She started to put her hand up.

But everybody would know then! They would know she was thinking about going to see a B movie. Sister would know. Bernadette would know. All her new friends would know. And suppose Father Deschamps said it *was* a mortal sin? Everybody would know she wanted to do something that was a mortal sin.

She sat back, dropping her hand on her lap. She couldn't ask him.

"Any more questions?" Father Deschamps said after a while.

No more hands were raised.

"Let's thank Father for a most instructive and *unusual* catechism lesson," said Sister, gliding to the front of the room.

"Thank you, Father."

"Thank you, children." Father raised his hand. *"In nomine Patris . . ."*

As the figure in the black cassock went out the door, Moira thought, I couldn't ask him here, but maybe I could ask him someplace else. A picture of the rectory, the old building where the priests lived, appeared in her mind. It was right next to the school. She had been inside only once, with her mother. The rectory smelled of furniture polish and real flowers and something she hadn't been able to identify that her mother said was ammonia for cleaning.

And it was dark inside, very dark, so dark the lights were on in the daytime. Just thinking about the rectory made little shivers go up and down her back.

She couldn't ask him in the rectory.

When the bell rang at three o'clock, the class filed into the cloakroom, row by row. As she picked up her lunch box, Moira accidentally crashed it against Mary Lou's pink one.

"Watch out!" cried Mary Lou, grabbing her lunch box. She inspected the pictures of movie stars that she had pasted on it.

Treat everybody the way you'd like to be treated yourself, thought Moira. Easy to say! But what if Father Deschamps had Mary Lou in front of him all day? Somehow, she found her lips stretching into what felt like the phoniest smile in the world. "I'm sorry," she heard herself saying. "Is it okay?"

"I guess so." Scowling, Mary Lou wiggled out of the cloakroom.

She had treated Mary Lou the way she'd like to be treated herself and Mary Lou didn't even notice, thought Moira.

After she waved good-bye to Bernadette and the other girls, Moira stood at the bus stop. Soon all the children who had come out of the school had disappeared. She turned her head. The rectory was right in back of the bus stop. If she went up to the door now, nobody would see her. If she talked to Father Deschamps now, nobody would know.

The three-story building seemed to be pulling her. Without willing it, she found herself walking slowly toward it. The front door was high and dark, with a metal knocker. She reached up to lift the knocker.

The windows on either side of the door were as dark as midnight. Inside the big dark house with the funny smells, Father Deschamps might be a different kind of priest than he was in their classroom today. He might start talking about damnation and dreadful torments and eternity. Eternity! She couldn't go inside. She had to go home.

The knocker slipped out of her hand. *Whump!* The sound of the knocker hitting the door echoed in the after-school stillness. Almost at once, the big door swung open noiselessly, as if someone had been waiting right inside.

An old woman stood there, a tall old woman with gray hair. She wore a dark dress and an apron. The housekeeper. Priests always had a housekeeper. Priests didn't have wives, but they didn't cook or wash clothes or take out the garbage, her mother said. The housekeeper did it. This housekeeper stared at her, unsmiling, and said, "Yes?"

"I'd like to talk to Father Deschamps," gasped a high voice that didn't sound like hers at all.

"He's saying his office. Come back at four o'clock." The door swung closed.

Relieved, she turned and walked away. He was saying the office, again, just the way he had been when they met in the graveyard. Priests had to say those prayers every day. Well, she couldn't wait until four o'clock anyway. Her mother would wonder where she was.

There was a big statue in the side yard of the rectory, a statue of St. Teresa. Her eyes were closed and she held up her arms to the sky. St. Teresa wasn't like Mary. The statue of Mary in church looked at you, smiling. Even the statue in the classroom seemed mildly interested in you. St. Teresa didn't look at you and she didn't smile. She was thinking about God. Sometimes, when she was thinking very hard about God, she had flown right up in the air. That was in this long, long book she was reading on St. Teresa for her report.

"Moira!"

Father Deschamps was coming toward her, carrying a black prayer book. He must have been in the backyard.

"Did you want to see me, Moira?"

No, she almost said. But Father Deschamps was smiling a little, looking just the way he had in the classroom. Maybe he didn't turn into a priest like Father Monahan until he actually went *inside* the rectory.

"Yes, Father. But the housekeeper said you were saying your office."

"I'll finish it later. Come on."

Were they going inside? No, he was walking toward the backyard. She let out her breath.

"Did you want to ask me something?" Father Deschamps looked down at her.

All of a sudden, she couldn't talk. Father Deschamps seemed friendly now, but what would he say if he knew she wanted to see a B movie, a movie Objectionable in Part for All?

"Is it something about the catechism lesson?" asked Father.

"No. It's about . . . about a movie." Her words spurted out the way water did when you turned it on hard. "Father, if somebody went to see a B movie, a B movie like *Gone With the Wind*, would that be a venial sin or a mortal sin?"

117

"Is that somebody a child?"

"Yes. It's . . . me. I'm reading *Gone With the Wind*! I'm almost done! It's the most wonderful book I've ever read!"

"Do you remember the three conditions for a mortal sin?" asked Father Deschamps.

"A grievous matter sufficient reflection and full consent of the will," she said all in one breath.

"Let's sit down here," said Father Deschamps, pointing to a stone bench. "Do you know what all of that means? I don't mean the catechism answer."

He didn't mean the catechism answer! He was always asking things that weren't in the catechism.

Moira wrinkled her forehead, thinking. "Sufficient reflection means thinking a lot. And full consent of the will means you know what you're doing. And a grievous matter . . ." Her nose began to itch. She grabbed the damp ball in her pocket and held it to her nose. What *was* a grievous matter? That's what she couldn't decide!

"Seeing a movie like *Gone With the Wind*—is that a grievous matter?" prompted Father.

"The Legion of Decency says you shouldn't see a B movie," said Moira, ending her answer with a sneeze.

"Bless you," said Father Deschamps. "Grievous means serious. But some things are more serious than others. Things the pope says about faith and morals—

those are serious. Things the Holy Scriptures say . . ." He looked down at her.

"Like the Ten Commandments," said Moira through her handkerchief. *"Very* serious."

"Very serious." Father nodded. "But movies . . ."

"Not so serious?" she asked.

"Not so serious," he agreed.

"But the Legion of Decency . . ."

"Your conscience is more important than the Legion of Decency," said Father Deschamps. "Ask your conscience whether you should see the movie or not."

Her conscience! She had never asked her conscience anything! People always told you what you ought to do. From the backyard, she could see a sliver of the street way down the block. A bus was moving slowly through the sliver as it made its way toward the rectory. "My bus!" she cried. "Thanks, Father!"

Running through the rectory yard, she felt as though her feet were pounding out a rhythm. Not serious—not serious—not serious. If seeing a movie wasn't serious, then it couldn't be a mortal sin! She wouldn't go to hell if she saw *Gone With the Wind*! She didn't have to worry about getting to confession right afterward! Not serious—not serious—not serious!

She was passing the statue of St. Teresa, who sometimes flew right up in the air when she thought about God. Moira felt almost as if she could fly now, too.

But when she was on the bus, she remembered the

rest of what Father Deschamps had said. Ask your conscience whether you should see the movie or not. But suppose you had never asked your conscience anything? Your conscience was probably just lying around inside, sleeping. She had to figure out how to wake it up. And she wasn't quite sure how you knew what your conscience decided, either. Did it have a voice, like the radio?

Staring out the window, she felt the sudden weight of responsibility. She couldn't look up the answer. She couldn't ask anyone what it was. It was up to her conscience to figure out what she should do.

12

I'd like one ticket for next Saturday's matinee of *Gone With the Wind*," breathed Moira.

"Only general admission left," said the lady behind the ticket window. "Side aisles. One dollar."

"Okay." She fumbled in her purse and pulled out the dollar bill.

The ticket didn't look anything like the regular tickets for the Lebanon Theater. This ticket said GONE WITH THE WIND in big letters. Below that it gave the date and the time of the show. Moira stared at the ticket in her hand. It was real! She was going! She would see it on Saturday afternoon, before Jane did!

Last night, she had put down all the facts about *Gone With the Wind* on a piece of paper to make it easy for her conscience. "Should I go?" she said aloud.

By the time she went to bed, there hadn't been any answer. But just before she fell asleep, she thought she heard a voice. "Go," the voice was saying. Her conscience? Well, if it wasn't her conscience, what else could it be?

After she got up this morning, she worked out the whole plan for seeing *Gone With the Wind*. She'd buy the ticket this morning, before she went to art school. Then, next Saturday, she'd start off just like she was going to art school. But she would go to the Lebanon Theater instead.

Her mother and father would never know.

And now she was walking toward St. Teresa's Rectory and the streetcar stop with the ticket in her purse. When she got near the rectory, she could see a girl standing at the streetcar stop. Bernadette. She waved.

"You always take the bus to here," said Bernadette as Moira came up to her.

"I had to get something in Lebanon." It wasn't a lie, either.

The streetcar was coming. They climbed on and sat in one of the double seats.

"I went to the Lebanon Theater last night with my mom and dad," said Bernadette. "They had the previews of *Gone With the Wind*!"

"I saw the previews, too!"

"Clark Gable is so handsome in it! I wish I could see the movie."

"Me, too," said Moira, patting her purse with the ticket inside. She couldn't tell Bernadette she was going to see the movie. Bernadette was so religious. She might think you shouldn't go see *Gone With the Wind* even if Father Deschamps said movies weren't serious. Even if he said a conscience was more important than the Legion of Decency.

It was safer to keep quiet.

"Last week, you said Scarlett went to Atlanta to get the money to save Tara," said Bernadette.

By the time they got to St. Luke's, Scarlett was married to her sister's boyfriend and having another baby. Going home, Moira continued the story.

"After Scarlett's married, she keeps right on working, even though everybody thinks it's the wrong thing to do. Well, one day Scarlett drives her carriage to the lumberyard by herself at night. These two bad men grab her . . ."

"Oh!"

"Yes, they grab her and they tear the whole front of her dress off! But she's rescued by Big Sam, who used to be a slave at Tara. Scarlett's husband gets together with Ashley and Rhett Butler and they kill the men. But Scarlett's husband gets killed, too."

"Oh! So Scarlett is a widow—again!"

"Yes. And Rhett proposes to her the day of the funeral!"

"How awful!" cried Bernadette, her eyes shining. "Do they get married?"

"Well, that's as far as I got because I have to read this long book on St. Teresa for my special report. It's due Monday." Moira sighed.

"I know. Sister's strict." Bernadette turned to look at Moira. "But she likes you."

"Likes me! She doesn't!" Moira shook her head hard.

"She does. She thinks you're smart. She thinks you have talent, too. For art."

Moira shook her head again, but slower. Sister had looked up her bus schedule. Sister had arranged for her to go to St. Luke's with Bernadette. Sister had asked if she left the lunchroom early. Sister was interested in her. Maybe Sister did like her! Moira looked at Bernadette out of the corner of her eye. Sister had done all those things, but somebody had seen her leave the lunchroom early. Somebody had seen her drawing. Somebody had seen her taking the bus. Bernadette?

Bernadette was smiling at her. "I forgot to tell you! I have this short book on St. Teresa! Come to confession with me when we get off the streetcar. Then we can go to my house and I'll give it to you."

Bernadette, thought Moira, returning the smile.

124

"Okay," she said. "But I don't have a hat." You had to cover your head when you went into a Catholic church. If you didn't, it was a sin.

"You can wear my veil," said Bernadette. "I'll use my handkerchief." She opened her tiny purse and took out a tiny package. Inside the package, neatly folded, was a white piece of veiling just big enough to cover your hair.

Didn't Bernadette ever forget anything? wondered Moira, accepting the veil.

It was late afternoon when they got back to Lebanon again. Outside the church, Bernadette secured the handkerchief to her head with a bobby pin. She loaned one to Moira for the veil. The church was dark and quiet inside. Dipping their hands in the holy water basin, they made the sign of the cross on their chests.

Bernadette pointed to Father Monahan's confessional. His name was on a lighted sign above the door. People were kneeling in the pews next to the confessional, awaiting their turn to go in.

Moira looked across the church to the other confessional. The sign above the door read: FATHER SCHMITT. He was the assistant to Father Monahan. Father Schmitt never seemed to listen in confession and he always gave the same penance, three Our Fathers and three Hail Marys. Rosemary Randolph told this joke about somebody who had murdered somebody and then went to confession to Father Schmitt. He gave him three Our Fathers and three Hail Marys.

But Moira preferred Father Schmitt to Father Monahan. Sometimes Father Monahan asked questions in confession, embarrassing questions. Moira pointed to Father Schmitt's confessional. Bernadette nodded.

There weren't as many people next to Father Schmitt's confessional, so soon Moira found herself inside the tiny, dark space. Father Schmitt rolled back the wooden cover that went over the window.

"Bless me, Father, for I have sinned . . ." began Moira.

Father Schmitt's head rested on one hand. Was he awake?

". . . and when my mother asked me to do the dishes, I said I had a sore throat, but I didn't. I'm very sorry for all my sins."

"Three Our Fathers and Three Hail Marys. Now say a good Act of Contrition."

He was awake. In minutes she was outside again, feeling relieved. She always felt that way when she came out of confession. Folding her hands, she walked toward Mary's altar to the left of the main altar. On one side of Mary's altar was a stand with rows of little candles. Most of them were burning, their tiny flames turning the red glass containers into red jewels.

Moira knelt down at the railing of the altar. Mary

held the baby Jesus in one arm, but she held the other out to the pews in front of her. Her plaster lips smiled. Moira bowed her head. "Hail Mary, full of grace . . ."

When she was finished with her penance, she looked up at the statue. Her thoughts rushed out the way they always did when she and Mary were together. Mary, I talked to Father Deschamps about seeing *Gone With the Wind*. It's a B, you know. Well, Father said I should ask my conscience what to do. So last night I asked it and just before I went to sleep I heard this voice saying, "Go." I thought the voice was my conscience. Was it? Anyway, Father Deschamps said movies aren't serious, so seeing a B movie couldn't be a mortal sin. Could it?

The plaster lips smiled.

I got the ticket this morning, Mary. It cost a dollar—that's four times as much as the regular Saturday matinee. It's for general admission, not a real reserved seat in the middle. A real reserved seat is *two* dollars, and besides, they didn't have any left. The ticket's in my purse. She patted the purse hanging on her shoulder.

Were the plaster lips smiling a little more? Sometimes she thought the smile got bigger after she talked to Mary. Somewhere there was this statue of Mary that cried tears—Sister Gabriel Mary had told them about it—so maybe a statue could smile more, too. Opening her purse, she brought out a dime. She dropped it in the slot in the middle of the candle rack. When she lit a candle, the tiny flame made the red glass container into another jewel.

She turned around. Bernadette was walking toward her, head down and hands folded. She slid into one of the pews in front of Mary's altar and buried her face in her hands. Moira slid into the pew from the other side.

Finally Bernadette stood up. They dipped their hands in the holy water basin again as they walked out of the church.

"My house is only a block and a half away," said Bernadette. They crossed the street at the light and walked along the sidewalk. After they turned at the first block, Bernadette said, "That's my house. The brick one with the porch."

The house was small and old and dark. They clattered up the wooden steps of the porch. Bernadette pushed open the screen door. "Mom? I'm home. I've got Moira Flynn from school with me."

The inside of the house was small and old and dark, too. On the wall was a picture of Mary with the baby Jesus. The woman who came out of the room at the back of the house wore a big apron that covered her top and bottom.

"Mom, this is Moira," said Bernadette, kissing the woman. "This is my mom."

"You want some lemonade?" asked Bernadette's

mother. "It's hot enough outside. Are we ever going to get fall?"

They took the lemonade back to Bernadette's bedroom, a tiny, dark room with only enough room for a single bed and a small chest of drawers and an even smaller desk. The pink spread was tightly pulled over the bed. Bernadette's notebook and schoolbooks were lined up on the desk. Her pencils and pens were in a glass. There wasn't a single thing that wasn't where it should be.

Bernadette was so neat, thought Moira.

Hanging over the bed was another holy picture, this one of the Sacred Heart. Christ was pointing to the heart, which you could see through his gown. The heart had a crown of thorns around it.

Bernadette picked a book out of a row on top of the chest of drawers. "Here it is. My brother gave it to me. He's in the seminary."

"It is short."

"There's a cover, too." Bernadette opened the bottom drawer of the chest.

Moira got a glimpse of a familiar scene. Scarlett O'Hara in front of Tara! "The *Gone With the Wind* paper-doll book!" cried Moira. "Do you play paper dolls?"

"Well, not anymore," said Bernadette, closing the drawer. "Here's the cover."

Not anymore. Jane didn't play paper dolls anymore,

either. They sat down side by side on the bed. Moira examined the book on St. Teresa.

"Do you like Ronald?" asked Bernadette suddenly.

Startled, Moira dropped the book into her lap. "Well . . ." she said, thinking that she did like Ronald, but maybe she shouldn't say so. Ronald was bad, and Bernadette was so religious. "Well, sort of," she said finally. "He's so funny."

"He is funny. Tom McNeilly says he's smart but he doesn't study. Tom studies a lot. Do you know he goes to mass every day? I see him there when I go."

Bernadette liked Tom! Moira stared at her, surprised. She hadn't thought Bernadette was interested in boys. She was so religious. And she liked Tom, of all people. Tom seemed so . . . unlikable. "You like Tom," said Moira.

Bernadette looked down at her lap. "Um-hmm. Do you know he's the tallest boy in both seventh grades? But he says he's going to be a priest."

"Oh." She could see Tom as a priest. If he was a priest he'd be able to tell people things all the time and they'd have to listen. Poor Bernadette. Well, Ronald wasn't going to be a priest, that was for sure.

Her eyes moved around the neat room. On the desk was another picture. Clark Gable, dressed as Rhett Butler. It looked like the picture from *Life* magazine.

"Clark Gable," she said, pointing.

"I cut it out of *Life*."

"I cut Vivien Leigh's picture out of *Life*. It's on my chest of drawers."

Bernadette was her friend now. She was nice, even if she was so religious. And she liked Clark Gable the same way Moira liked Ashley. This was Bernadette's only chance to see Clark Gable in *Gone With the Wind*. She had to tell Bernadette about what Father Deschamps had said. Maybe they could even go to see *Gone With the Wind* together next Saturday!

Moira leaned toward Bernadette and spoke in a whisper. "Do you promise not to tell anyone what I tell you?"

Bernadette opened her eyes and looked surprised. "Okay," she whispered back. "Cross my heart, hope to die." Her hand made a cross on her chest.

"I talked to Father Deschamps yesterday," whispered Moira. "At the rectory." She looked up to make sure the door was closed. "I asked him if seeing a B movie like *Gone With the Wind* would be a venial sin or a mortal sin."

"What did he say?"

"He asked me what the three conditions for a mortal sin are. You know."

"Sufficient reflection, full consent of the will, and a grievous matter."

"Well, *he* said that things the Holy Father says

about faith and morals are serious. And things in Holy Scriptures. But the movies aren't serious like that." She sat back on the bed.

"What do you mean?" whispered Bernadette.

"Well if it isn't a grievous matter, it can't be a mortal sin if you do it, can it? Oh—and he said your conscience is more important than the Legion of Decency!"

Bernadette's voice rose. "More important than the Legion of Decency! But the Legion of Decency has all these bishops . . ."

"Shhhhh! Cross my heart, hope to die, that's what he said." Moira made a cross over her chest. "Look!" She opened her purse and took out the ticket.

Bernadette took the ticket. " *'Gone With the Wind,'* " she read. " 'Saturday, one P.M. One dollar.' You're going to see it!"

"Yes, next Saturday instead of going to art school. And you can go, too! They had some general-admission tickets left. But we shouldn't tell anybody. Because, well, some people, they might not understand. It'll be our secret."

Bernadette turned to look at the photograph of Clark Gable. The bedroom was very quiet. Then, leaping up, Bernadette opened the top drawer of the desk. "I have five dollars saved!" she cried, waving some bills. "I'll get a ticket tomorrow!"

"We'll go see it together!"

They hugged each other, laughing.

13

So I'm taking something out of my purse in the kitchen," whispered Bernadette, "and my ticket for *Gone With the Wind* falls out! My mother says, 'What's that for?' "

Moira gasped, putting down her empty lunch box. "What did you say?"

"I knew I couldn't lie if she asked me what it was! That'd be a sin. I felt like I was having a heart attack! But just then—"

"I see some empty seats," called Sister's voice from the front of the room.

They rushed out of the cloakroom. "The phone rang. She forgot about the ticket," whispered Bernadette before she went to her desk.

Relieved, Moira sank down at her own desk. Sister was gliding up and down in front of the room, pointer in her hand. Footsteps, whispers, and desk sounds died away as Sister whirled to face the class.

"We're going to have a special visit from Father Deschamps this afternoon, boys and girls," said Sister.

A low buzz.

"That's enough!" Sister pulled down the geography chart. "Today we'll talk about Australia and New Zealand," she said, pointing to two shapes at the lower right-hand corner of the map. "What are the principal products of Australia?"

The usual hands went up. Moira wiped her nose. Hot windy days like this were bad for allergies. The things that made you sneeze were flying around.

"Tom," said Sister without even looking around.

"Wool and mutton," said Tom. "Mutton, that's sheep meat," he said, looking at the class. "You see, Australia is like a desert in the middle, so they can't grow crops. They raise sheep."

"Baaaaaaa," said a voice.

Smothered laughter from the class.

Sister whirled, her eyes on Ronald Colligan. But Ronald was sitting with his hands folded on his desk, his expression very solemn. There was nothing to show that Ronald had said, "Baaaaa." But of course he had, thought Moira, hiding her smile with her hand.

Sister tapped her hand with the pointer. "Correct,"

she said in a soft voice. "Perhaps, Ronald, you'd like to tell us the principal cities of Australia."

"Um," said Ronald, wrinkling his forehead. "Um . . ."

"Everyone was to read the section on Australia and New Zealand in the geography book last night," said Sister in the same soft voice. "So I'm sure you know them." The pointer tapped faster. "What are the principal cities of Australia, Ronald?" she barked in a loud voice that made everyone jump.

"Um, Birmingham . . ."

Laughter.

"Birmingham is thousands of miles north of Australia," said Sister, gliding toward Ronald's desk with her pointer raised. "In England. Last week you didn't know the biggest river in France. The week before, you couldn't remember the capital of Spain!"

In the corner next to the window, the statue of Mary seemed to gaze at Ronald with disbelief. The capital of Spain was easy, thought Moira. So were the other questions. Didn't Ronald ever study?

Sister whirled again, heading away from Ronald. Moira let out her breath. "Children, those in St. Teresa's School who do not wish to take advantage of the wonderful privilege of a Catholic education will be sent . . . somewhere else!" The pointer came down on Sister's desk, making everybody jump.

Silence enveloped the classroom, silence so complete that the knock on the door sounded like thunder. Everybody jumped again.

The door opened and Father Deschamps came in. The class scrambled to its feet. "Good afternoon, Father."

"Good afternoon, boys and girls. Please be seated." He looked at the geography chart. "It looks as though I'm interrupting a geography lesson."

"An interruption from you is always welcome, Father," said Sister, giving him one of her small smiles.

Father Deschamps faced the class. "I've come to say good-bye to you, boys and girls."

A murmur swept through the class, a murmur that died as Sister flashed a blue warning with her eyes.

"I've only been at St. Teresa's a short time, but that's been long enough for me to feel at home here," said Father Deschamps. "There are so many good people here. I know I'm going to miss them. But I feel I have to leave."

He walked up and down in front of the room. "The world is facing a very serious crisis today. You know what I'm talking about, don't you?"

Tom raised his hand. "The war, Father."

"Yes, the war. Do you know our country has over a million men and women in the armed forces today? And tens of thousands are added each month. Someday soon, our country will probably be part of the war.

It will be the biggest war we've ever fought. I feel I have to help our country, boys and girls. I'm going to become a chaplain for the U.S. Army."

Father Deschamps was leaving, thought Moira. Leaving forever. It wasn't fair! Just when she found a priest she liked, a priest she could talk to, he had to leave. And then another thought crept into her mind. There *was* going to be a war. Her father was right. Her mother was wrong.

"I'd like to hear from any of the students at St. Teresa's who would like to write to me," Father Deschamps was saying. "This will be my address."

He chalked an address with lots of numbers and letters on the board. "I promise to write back," he said.

Father talked to Sister in a low voice. Then he looked at the class and raised his hand for the blessing. *"In nomine Patris ..."*

The door closed after him.

"Class, let us say a special prayer for Father Deschamps and for all the men and women in our armed forces," said Sister. She clasped her hands in front of her. "Our Father ..."

When the prayer was finished, Moira wrote down the address in her notebook. She would write Father, she thought. Maybe she would even tell him about seeing *Gone With the Wind* this Saturday. A sneeze was coming! She jammed her handkerchief against her nose. Lots of times that didn't work, but this time it did.

Sister had picked up a pile of papers from her desk. "I'm passing out maps of Australia and New Zealand, boys and girls. Indicate on these the major geographical features of each country, including the biggest cities. Do not look at your geography book! This will be a test and it will count toward your grade in geography."

A low groan.

"That's enough! You have one half hour. Those who are unable to complete their map will do it after school with their geography book open." Sister sat down at her desk.

A surprise test. And Sister had done it just to catch Ronald. It was mean. Moira looked at the map passed back to her. Then she bent over it, her pencil working rapidly. She shot a glance toward Ronald. Ronald was just sitting there, not writing anything. A fly had landed on her map. She swatted it with her pencil, but of course she missed. Flies were fast. There were other flies in the room. She could hear them buzzing loudly.

"Eeeeek!"

Moira looked up. A huge black bee was buzzing through the room. It flew low over Row E, making everyone in that row duck.

"Just ignore the bee," said Sister. "It will go away."
Moira put another name on the map.

"Get away!" Rosemary Randolph in Row E raised her paper to fend off the bee. Ronald swatted at it with his ruler.

"Children! It's only a bee!" Sister frowned at Row E.

Suddenly the bee, having evaded the ruler, turned. The class drew in its breath like one person. The bee was now flying in the direction of the big front desk! A beeline, thought Moira, watching the big black creature's unwavering flight toward the desk and its occupant. Sister glared at the bee, but it paid no attention. On it flew until it was over the desk, heading right toward Sister.

Ronald Colligan stood up, ruler in hand. The bee was circling Sister's head now, its buzzing as loud as an airplane in the quiet room. Ronald walked toward the desk, raising his ruler. Sister, as still as the statue of Mary in the corner, watched Ronald. Moira tried to read her expression. Scared? Mad? Confused? Some of all of those, maybe.

A gasp from the class. The bee had landed on the shiny white part of Sister's headdress! The bee looked like a huge black ink blot now. Slowly the blot moved down the shiny white field toward Sister's forehead. Sister didn't move.

Ronald Colligan put down his ruler on the desk. He held his arm straight out. Leaning forward, he closed his first two fingers over the big black blot.

Tom jumped up. "Come on!" he cried, racing to the door. He threw it open.

Ronald, still holding the bee at arm's length, followed Tom out the door. Their shoes clattered down the steps.

A sigh whispered through the class, but for once Sister didn't cry, "That's enough!" She didn't say anything at all as she raised one hand to the shiny white part of her headdress. Her face had no expression. The hand dropped. Then she jumped up and walked to the door. They heard her heavy black shoes clattering down the steps.

Everyone started to talk at once. Moira was surprised to find out that she and Mary Lou were talking.

"Did you ever see anything *like* that?" asked Mary Lou, wiggling her shoulders in her new white blouse. "Ron's cute, don't you think?" She smiled, her nice smile this time.

"Uh-huh," agreed Moira, feeling a little worried. If Mary Lou liked Ronald . . .

More footsteps, this time coming back up. Sister glided through the door, followed by Tom and Ronald. Ronald! Had he been stung? He looked just the same. Ronald was so brave! And so cute!

"We let the bee go outside," announced Tom. "Ron didn't even get stung. It was a bumblebee, the biggest U.S. bee. I think it was a female because the abdomen—"

"Tom," said Sister. "Sit down. Sit down and shut up."

Moira and Mary Lou looked at each other, mouths open. Sister had said "shut up"! Sisters never said shut up! She had said it to Tom, too—the smartest student in the class!

"And he's going to be a *priest,*" whispered Moira. Mary Lou's mouth opened even wider.

Tom sat down. Ronald sat down, too.

Sister stood in front of Ronald's desk. She clasped her hands in front of her. "Ronald has done a very brave thing," she said. "He might have been stung. I would like to thank you publicly, Ronald."

Ronald stared at his desk. He looked embarrassed, thought Moira. Maybe he didn't know how to act when people said something good about him, because they usually said something bad.

Sister picked up the map of Australia and New Zealand on Ronald's desk. "Rosemary! Will you collect the maps, please?"

"But we aren't done, Sister," said Rosemary.

"Collect the maps, please. We will have this test Monday. I hope you will all study." Her eyes rested for a moment on Ronald. "For the rest of the after-noon, we are going to read a book."

A murmur from the class, but Sister didn't say any-thing. They hardly ever read a real book, thought Moira. What book could it be? Sister went to her desk and took a book out of one of the drawers. She handed the book to Teresa Sullivan in the first seat in Row A.

"Read the first page, Teresa, then pass the book to Michael behind you," said Sister.

The cover of the book was familiar. *Father Damien of Molokai!* Just her luck! They were actually going to read a real book and it had to be *Father Damien of Molokai,* a book she'd already read. And it wasn't even a good book.

As the reading began, Sister walked to the win-dows and stared out. Watching Sister from the cor-ner of her eye, Moira could see her wrinkled forehead. And then she saw Sister turn her head just a little bit so that she could see Ronald. The wrinkles in the white forehead got deeper.

When the three o'clock bell rang, Sister stopped Ronald as he was rushing to the cloakroom. They were still talking when Moira left the room. Outside the building, Bernadette and Teresa joined Moira.

"Can you believe picking up a bee with your fin-gers?" asked Teresa.

"It was so incredibly brave," said Bernadette.

"I wonder how Sister feels," said Moira.

"Embarrassed," said Bernadette.

"Sorry," said Teresa.

"Mixed-up," said Moira. "She doesn't know why he did it."

"Hasn't this been one weird day?" asked Bernadette. "First Father Deschamps going into the army and then Ronald saving Sister from the bee!"

"It's one of ten weirdest days at St. Teresa's," said Teresa.

Laughing, they walked up the wide sidewalk together. Moira waved good-bye at the bus stop. After almost everyone had left the school, she saw a figure come out the front door. Her heart jumped. Ronald. He walked up the wide sidewalk to the street.

"Hi, Moira."

"Hi, Ronald." She swallowed. It was so hard to talk to boys. Boys were so different! "Ronald, it was so brave of you to take the bee off Sister," she said quickly in a small voice. "*Especially* when she's so mean to you."

"I've picked up bees before," said Ronald.

"Have you?"

"Yeah. You've got to know how to do it. Hey, you go to the Lebanon Theater, don't you?"

"Yes."

"I'll see you there sometime," he said as he walked away.

She watched his disappearing figure. What did he mean, he'd see her there? Would he sit with her? Talk

143

to her? You never knew what boys meant. Jane would know—maybe. And even if she didn't know, Jane would want to talk about it.

The Sunrise Hills bus was pulling into the curb. Moira climbed on. She would call Jane tonight.

14

Smiling, Moira put down the hall telephone. Jane said Ronald liked her. Jane said to come over Sunday and they'd talk about it. Jane said she'd tell her about how one of the twins, the cutest one, had actually asked her something.

A woman's voice was singing "God Bless America" on the radio. Kate Smith. Kate Smith was the only one who sang "God Bless America."

Her mother was listening to Kate Smith in the living room. Her father was reading in the dining room. Sometimes Moira listened to Kate Smith, but tonight she wanted to read *Gone With the Wind*. She was almost finished and tomorrow she'd be seeing the movie! She flew up the stairs to her room.

She hadn't thought of it until now, but Jane hadn't

mentioned that she should bring her paper dolls on Sunday. Every time she went to Jane's, she brought her paper dolls. Sitting down on the rug in front of her chest of drawers, Moira opened the bottom drawer. The book with Vivien Leigh and Clark Gable standing in front of the big white house with pillars was on top.

She picked up the book. Inside, the Scarlett doll wore only her white chemise and pantalets. Moira hunted through the pile of cut-out dresses. She fastened the paper tabs of the white gown with the little flowers to the doll's shoulders.

Ashley was already wearing a suit.

"Ashley, you do care—you do, don't you?" the Scarlett doll asked.

"Yes, I care."

Bernadette said she didn't play paper dolls anymore. Moira put the Scarlett doll, still dressed in the white gown with the little flowers, back in the book. She placed the Ashley doll right next to her. Then she closed the cover with Scarlett and Rhett standing in front of the big white house with pillars. She would keep her paper dolls safe in their books and look at them sometimes, all by herself.

Closing the drawer gently, she stood up.

In the mirror over the dressing table, she saw a serious-looking girl with brown hair that hung limply around her face. Maybe she should try pulling the sides of her hair up again the way Jane did. She still had Jane's bobby pins. She had both sides up when the phone rang. She flew down the steps, but her father got there first.

"For you, Moira."

She picked up the phone. "Hello?"

"Moira?" It was Bernadette's voice. "Oh, Moira, I can't go."

Something in Moira's stomach went *boinnnnnggg*. She sank down on the step and clutched the phone to her cheek. *"Why?"*

"My brother, the one who's in the seminary, he's here for the weekend. I showed him my ticket . . ."

"Why?"

"Because . . . because I wasn't *sure*. And he said, he said . . ." Bernadette sniffed.

"What?"

"He said that a Catholic conscience based on the teachings of the Church should command us to avoid near occasions of sin like a B movie," said Bernadette very fast. "He said a B movie tempts us to break God's laws. He said . . ."

Bernadette's voice went on and on. Moira scrunched her eyes closed. She never should have told Bernadette. Bernadette was too religious!

"And he said, he said, a really good Catholic

wouldn't *want* to see a B movie!" Bernadette's voice ended in a kind of sob.

Kate Smith's powerful voice was singing "When the Moon Comes over the Mountain" in the living room. Moira found herself concentrating on the song, even though she didn't like it.

"Moira? Moira, are you still there? I took the ticket back already. I'm sorry."

Moira's mind seemed to shift into gear. Bernadette had told their secret to her brother! She hated Bernadette! And if her mother hadn't been listening to Kate Smith in the living room and her father hadn't been reading a book in the dining room, she would have told Bernadette how much she hated her! But as it was, all she could do was whisper, "I hear you!" and slam down the phone.

"Margaret, are you still listening to that show?" called her father's voice. "I want to hear the news."

"The Kate Smith show is over, Dave. Come on in."

Moira ran back up the stairs. Bernadette was too religious! She should have known Bernadette wouldn't go! She never should have told her about going to the movie. Moira felt her throat tighten. Because now she was wondering if she, Moira, should go herself. A really good Catholic, Bernadette's brother said, wouldn't even *want* to see a B movie. And she wanted to see it so much.

She dropped down on the bed. Maybe she wasn't a good Catholic. Maybe that was why she wanted to see the movie so much.

There was something hard underneath her. She stood up. *Gone With the Wind* was lying on the bed. She sat back down and opened the book. She wanted to get out of her own world, where everything was going so badly, and into the world of Scarlett and Rhett and Ashley and Melanie. There wasn't much left to read.

When her mother and father came up to bed, she was almost finished.

"You go to bed now, Moira," said her mother. "It's ten o'clock and you have to go to art school tomorrow."

"Okay." She opened the drawer of her dressing table and took out a small flashlight. She switched off the lamp on her dressing table. Under the quilt, the flashlight's small beam illuminated half a dozen lines at a time. She turned the pages rapidly.

" 'It's you I want. Take me with you.'

" 'No,' he said."

Tears ran down Moira's face. She turned the last page.

" 'I'll think of it all tomorrow, at Tara.... Tomorrow I'll think of some way to get him back. After all, tomorrow is another day.' "

It was over. And Scarlett and Rhett weren't together. Oh, how could that be? It was so sad. But somehow, it was right. She turned off the flashlight and put it and the book on her dressing table. It was the best book she'd ever read. Never, ever would she read a book as wonderful as this one.

But should she see the movie? "A really good Catholic . . ."

She closed her eyes.

When she woke up, sunlight was falling on her red and white quilt. *Gone With the Wind* was on the dressing table. She had finished it. And the movie, the movie for which she had a ticket, was today. Last week, after she asked her conscience about seeing the movie, she had heard a voice saying, "Go." But last night she hadn't heard the voice.

She got out of bed and sniffed. Her nose felt okay. Maybe this would be a good day for allergies.

In the kitchen, her mother put a bowl of cereal in front of Moira. Then her mother sat down at the table and picked up the newspaper. "Snow," she said. "There's snow in the Soviet Union already."

"In October?" Moira looked out the window. It was so warm and sunny here that Sister Gabriel Mary almost got stung by a bee. It was so warm she still had her allergies. But in the Soviet Union, there was snow. And war. The war! Father Deschamps was going into the army. Last night, she had told her parents about the bee and forgotten to tell them about Father Deschamps.

"Father Deschamps is going in the army," she said. "To be a chaplain."

"He is?"

"He says we're going to get into the war."

The back door opened. Mr. Flynn came in with a basket of tomatoes.

"Father Deschamps is leaving to be an army chaplain, Dave. He told the children we're going to be in the war."

"Well, Father's got the right idea," said Mr. Flynn. "We have to do something to help England stop that Hitler. The Germans are almost in Moscow now." He held a tomato up to the light from the window.

Moira and her mother stared at each other. Now Daddy wants to help England, thought Moira, amazed.

"The morning paper says it's snowing in the Soviet Union, Dave."

"Snowing? That's good! Remember what happened to Napoleon."

"What?" asked Moira.

"Napoleon invaded Russia—that's what they called it then—just like Hitler. But Napoleon had to retreat when the snows came. He lost a lot of his men. And then he lost the war."

We really are going to be in a war, thought Moira. Would they have air raids here, too? Would there be tanks? And dead people? War was serious. What had Father Deschamps said? Some things were serious. Some weren't.

Movies weren't serious. Suddenly she knew what she was going to do this afternoon. She hadn't heard a voice. Maybe she hadn't heard a voice before, either. But she knew what she was going to do. She had to call Bernadette first, though.

When her father had gone back to the garden and her mother was listening to the kitchen radio, she picked up the phone. Bernadette's voice answered.

"Bernadette? It's me. I'm going to the movie. By myself."

"Oh."

"I thought a lot about it and I think my conscience says to go."

"Oh. Are you mad?"

"No . . ." It was true. She wasn't mad anymore. Bernadette was nice even if she was so religious, even if she had told the secret to her brother. If it weren't for Bernadette—and Sister—she still wouldn't have any friends at St. Teresa's. "I'll tell you all about the movie," she said. "*If* you promise not to tell anyone, because . . . you know."

"Yes. I won't, cross my heart."

When it was time to leave, Moira picked up her art folder.

"What are you going to do today in art school?" asked her mother.

"I don't know. Sister Dymphna decides what we do." The first lie today. There would be so many others.

"Let's look at what you do when you get home, okay?"

"Um . . . okay." Another complication!

She walked toward the bus stop. Jane and Sally would be going to the movie together tonight. It wouldn't be as much fun going by herself. When you were with somebody, you got to poke them and whisper to them and hold on to them in the scary parts. And best of all, you got to talk about the movie right afterward. Jane and Sally would talk about the movie over sodas.

It was too early when she got to the Lebanon Theater to go inside. So she went to the library, which was only a block away. The library had long tables. She would draw something here, thought Moira. She would draw something here and tell her mother she'd done it at art school. A lie. She looked around. There was a bunch of flowers on the librarian's desk.

She would draw that. She opened her folder of art supplies.

When she looked at her watch, it was twelve-fifteen, time to go.

The whole lobby of the Lebanon Theater was full of people when she got there. At twelve-thirty, the doors opened. Inside the theater, it was so crowded that Moira couldn't even see the popcorn machine.

"General admission, side aisles," an usher kept saying.

She couldn't stop for popcorn anyway. She had to find a seat on the side aisle. She trotted toward the right-hand aisle, her favorite aisle. It was farther away from the door, so not so many people used it.

Doggone! All the aisle seats were taken. No, there was one left, about two-thirds of the way down! She began to run, zigzagging around people in the aisle.

But just as she reached the seat, somebody coming *up* the aisle slid in front of her and plopped down right in the seat. *Her* seat!

Indignantly, Moira stared at the somebody. A lady . . .

"Mom!"

"Moira!"

"I thought you were at home!"

"I thought you were at art school!"

Thoughts batted around Moira's brain like a fly on a window. How could her mother be here, ready to see a movie that was Objectionable in Part for All? That meant adults, too.

"Is this seat taken?" asked a lady, pointing to the seat next to Mrs. Flynn.

"No. Yes! Moira, sit here in my seat, you're shorter. I'll sit next to you."

Moira slid into the aisle seat. It was a wonderful seat. They were close, but not too close, and there was nobody in front of her at all. She would be able to see everything. She looked up at her mother. Her mother was staring straight ahead, her lips tight, her eyebrows pulled together. Was she mad?

"Mom? Are you mad?"

"Mad?" Mrs. Flynn looked down at her daughter. "No." She sighed. "Oh, Moira. I wanted to see this movie so much. I didn't tell your father I was going. I didn't tell anyone." She sighed again. "I should have known I couldn't keep it a secret. And now *you* know." Mrs. Flynn shook her head.

Her mother wanted to see the movie, too. As much as she did. Maybe more! "Mom, I asked Father Deschamps if it was a mortal sin to see *Gone With the Wind* and he said that for a mortal sin, you have to have a serious matter and a movie isn't really serious, besides your conscience . . ."

Mrs. Flynn patted Moira's hand. "Oh, shush, Moira. We'll think about it tomorrow."

Where had she heard that before?

The curtain was opening. A newsreel? Previews? No, a lion was roaring, the lion that roared before

155

the MGM movies started! And now the music was playing, the music from *Gone With the Wind*! The movie was starting right now!

Her mother's hand squeezed hers as the words *Gone With the Wind* filled the whole screen, the whole world.